Blood Feather Awakens

By
R.W.K. Clark

Published in the United States by Clarkltd.
Po Box 45313 Rio Rancho, NM 87174
info@clarkltd.com

Edition 1
United States Copyright Office
TX8-283-220 June 2016

Library of Congress Control Number: 2017907156

International Standard Book Numbers
ISBN-13: 978-0692734087 (Paperback)
ISBN-13: 978-1948312189 (Paperback)
ISBN-13: 978-1948312172 (Hardcover)
ASIN: B01GQBSZNK

/200801

PRAISES FOR BLOOD FEATHER AWAKENS

"Definitely check out this book with its interesting prehistoric spin."
— *Bryantwright on barnesandnoble*

"I tell you this, when you get to the end...bam! Didn't see that coming."
— *Kay on Amazon*

"Plenty of suspense, romance, and just the right amount of twists."
— *Yania on Amazon*

"Prehistoric angle really added even more interest to the book and kept me reading."
— *Freespirit on amazon*

"Grabs you by the throat and doesn't let you go."
— *Samanthaenq on barnesandnoble*

"Full of action, love, horror, lust, and danger. A spine-chilling read."
— *Lara on Amazon*

"A fun fast paced adventure."
— *Amazon Customer*

"This is a must-read!"
— *Jenalbc on barnesandnoble*

"A twist that really pulled my feathers."
— *Sasha R. Robertson on amazon AU*

"Combining romance, horror, and action, this book has it all!"
— *Ronyline on alibris*

"A very entertaining read, I most definitely recommend."
— *Cadenroberts on barnesandnoble*

"It was an amazing suspenseful thriller."
— *Clarence L. Daniels on amazon CA*

"I was on edge and could not stop reading."
— *Amazon Customer*

"I absolutely loved this novel!"
— *Rhodorah on barnesandnoble*

"Definitely a great summer read."
— *Brynsgreen on barnesandnoble*

"I would definitely recommend this one."
— *Kindle Edition UK*

"What an incredible read!"
— *Tyler Moore on Amazon*

CONTENTS

ACKNOWLEDGMENTS

I dedicate this novel to my wonderful readers and for all the amazing people I've met and those I haven't. To my family and loved ones, all your support will not be forgotten.

This book was made possible by reviews from readers like you.

Thank you

R.W.K. Clark

PROLOGUE

2.6 Million Years Ago…

The sky was growing dark, and the moon was blood-red. The jungle was eerily silent; nothing was stirring. Rather, every animal looked to the sky, frozen in place, with fear in their eyes.

In the distance, far off amidst the stars, was the streak of light. It grew closer, closer, and even closer still.

The mother bird shifted her attention to a large bush sitting about five feet from her. Beneath the bush, hidden from sight, was her nest, which held three eggs: her young. She was destined to have only three in her life cycle. Her only mission was to ensure their survival, and right now all she knew was that the light streaking toward Earth through the sky was threatening that mission. She looked one more time upward before leaping toward the bush. Her instincts kicked in and began to tell her what to do.

Her eggs were large, about eight inches in diameter, and they were quite beautiful, almost holographic, sharing blues, reds, yellows, and greens. She could not carry them all at once, so she grasped the edge of her massive nest in her razor-sharp beak and began to pull it out from under the bush. There was a tree with a hollow spot at its base. Her instincts told her to get her eggs to that hole; they would be safe there.

As she dragged her nest across the jungle floor, the light in the sky grew ever closer, and now it was giving off an audible howl. She continued to drag her nest, struggling with its weight, toward the hole in the base of the tree. The other animals which occupied the jungle were beginning to panic. They ran away from the danger to what they thought would be safety, but the bird knew that nothing was going to save them. All she could do was try to protect the young entrusted to her.

She got to the hole and looked up at the sky again. Now the light was gigantic, and the noise it was giving off was deafening. It would reach them any minute. She grabbed the largest of her eggs with two hand-like appendages which grew from her wings, allowing her to get a firm grip on whatever she chose. Right now she chose her eggs. She was beginning to panic a bit herself, and she tossed her egg into the dark hole in the tree and turned her attention back to the other two. The egg bounced slightly in the darkness and settled into a large puddle of thick yellowish sap which had pooled there. It sank into the puddle until it was eventually submerged in the sap.

The female bird reached for the second egg, but the brightness from the thing in the sky blinded her, and the sound of it surrounded her. She stumbled a bit, then fell over on top of the nest and the eggs inside of it. She began to tremble violently, and even her instincts shut themselves off at that point.

The large asteroid broke into the Earth's atmosphere then, and it overwhelmed everything with its size and sound. All of the animals and dinosaurs froze in panic, bracing themselves for their doom. The asteroid hit with such force that it vaporized everything in its path, from the animals to the trees, and it boiled the waters that had once taken care of the life that surrounded it.

But the egg in the sap remained intact, and time passed while nature took its course…

Four years ago, Peru

At first, the tremors were so slight that a human would have hardly noticed it, but they didn't stay that way.

The wildlife in that remote area of the Amazon felt it, though. Not only did they feel it, they knew there was more to come, and they began to scramble to save their own lives. The ground beneath their feet began to shake violently, and in many areas, it even split open and swallowed them whole.

In a small cave in the side of a cliff along the river, there was a stream, and it began to bubble as the rock and waters shook. Suddenly an object encased in a hard substance popped up from the waters. As the ground began to shake with more insistence and determination, it bounced against the dirt and rock of the cave. Suddenly it was rolling along the cave floor with no rhyme or reason, and it rolled along clumsily until it hit the wall of the cave hard. The substance which it was encased in had been softened by the waters which held it, and now it shattered like so much glass and fell away from the treasure inside.

It was a large egg, with a multi-colored pattern that seemed almost three-dimensional in appearance.

The tremors grew even more violent, and the egg rolled and bounced to and fro aimlessly until finally it rolled down a slight slope and rolled out of the cave completely. It continued to be guided by the shaking, taking what seemed to be a predetermined path to nowhere. The sun hit it, and the colors on the shell of the egg danced with great joy.

Suddenly the tremors stopped. The animals living in the jungle were loud and noisy, and there was nothing but chaos. But the egg settled into a groove in the dirt, protected from sight by its own appearance. It looked like nothing more than a rare and beautiful rock.

It settled into its new home, and the sun beat down on it, warming its surface greatly, and promising to hatch the bird living inside.

CHAPTER 1

Present day

Sam Daniels sat in the passenger side of the tour vehicle in silence, cleaning the lens on his camera and assembling it in preparation for all of the beauty he would be capturing. It was his third trip into this part of the Amazon jungles, and because he was familiar with the wildlife and greenery, he was excited about the pictures he would take. His driver, Rico, drove the car, which bounced around as they went deeper and deeper into the jungle. He was puffing on a stinky cigar as he struggled with the vehicle to keep it on the trail.

"Dang, Rico," Sam hollered, "why do you have to indulge in those smelly things?" He waved the smoke away from his face and shook his head.

Rico glanced over at him and snickered. "Why you worry about what I do?" he asked in broken English. "You worry about pictures. I worry about me."

Sam had been using Rico as his driver ever since his first trip into the jungle and the two men got along well. They formed a solid bond during his first trip when Sam fell into a shallow sinkhole, and Rico had rescued him. Ever since that day the two men had had a solid rapport that made for a good working relationship.

The car continued to bounce down the road as Sam finished dealing with his camera equipment. He laid it in his lap and took a long drink from his water bottle as he looked around at the emerald-green plants they were passing. He loved coming here, and he looked forward to it over all the other places he photographed.

The first two trips Sam took were pretty basic. He had come the first time only to photograph the land itself. He'd gotten amazing shots of the plant life and landscape, and he'd ended up selling them to *Planet Geographic*, which was groundbreaking for him. His second venture into the jungles had involved photographing the local peoples and the villages they lived in; those photos had been purchased by *World Magazine*. While he'd enjoyed both of those trips immensely, neither of them had really fulfilled his true desire: photographing the breathtaking wildlife.

Now he was back to do just that, and he found that he was beside himself with anticipation. He loved animals, and since he had finally gotten the attention of a couple of the most prolific periodicals in print, he was sure he could astound and impress with the pictures he was planning to take.

During his twenty-eight years on Earth, Sam had wanted to do only one thing: take pictures. He'd started at the tender age of nine with a film camera that his grandmother had purchased for him. She too had been a photographer, and it was she who had whetted his appetite for it. He'd used that camera for five years until his grandmother gifted him one for his thirteenth birthday. It was considered at the time a top-of-the-line consumer DSLR. Although it was not a professional grade, it had the features of manual mode and to Sam that had been the important part.

While other kids were climbing trees, building forts, and picking on girls, he was getting shots of anything he could find that would sit still for him, and some that wouldn't. He would show his pictures to his grandmother only, mostly because she was the only one who was interested in them. His parents both had professional careers that took up nearly all of their time, and he hardly ever saw them, much less shared his interests. They didn't have time for things they considered 'trivialities.'

So Sam would share his shots with his grandmother, and she would give him feedback and advice on how to be even better. He took everything she said and applied it. He treasured his relationship with her above all others, and when it came to photography, he considered her to be a deity.

By the time he turned fourteen she had begun helping him contribute his work to a variety of magazines. If he had shots of neighborhood animals or animals that lived in the woods surrounding his neighborhood he would contribute them to *Ranger Magazine*. If he shot plants or flowers, he would contribute to nature periodicals which focused on those topics, and his photos sold pretty well for his age.

But when Sam turned seventeen, his grandmother

had a stroke. She lost all functionality on the right side of her body, and she could no longer speak. His parents put her in a local nursing facility, and every day after school Sam would visit her and show her his most recent pictures. She could no longer give him advice, and doctors and nurses told him they didn't even believe she knew what she was looking at, but Sam could tell that she did, so he persisted. He knew by the way her eyes would light up that she knew exactly what was going on.

She passed away just after his eighteenth birthday, and it was one of the single most painful experiences of his life. He had been tempted to put his camera away forever; he didn't believe he could enjoy photography if he couldn't share it with her. He ignored his camera for all of two weeks, and it felt like he was dying inside. Finally, he determined that he would go on, and he would do it for his grandmother, in honor of their relationship. He went to California and studied photography at San Francisco's Academy of Art University's School of Photography, and it turned out to be the wisest move he had ever made.

∞

Now he bounced along in the beat-up SUV, tooling down the dirt roads of the Amazon with Rico and his smelly cigar, and he smiled to himself. He would have never been complete if he had given up photography altogether. Sam knew he was doing exactly what he was created to do. He would stop taking pictures when they pried his camera from his cold, dead hands.

Rico slowed the vehicle and steered it to the side of the road, pulling it off the main path to allow others to pass. He turned to Sam and took a long pull off his cigar and blew the smoke in Sam's face. Sam gave an exaggerated cough and gagged, which brought a smile to Rico's face.

"You ready?" he asked Sam. "We can go on foot from here."

Sam nodded his head yes and hung his now-professional-grade DSLR camera around his neck. Then he double-checked his bag to make sure he had everything he needed: his rain cover, extra batteries, a couple of spare memory cards, his tripod, hex keys, his pocket tool, and binoculars. He had a map of the area they were visiting, but Rico was in charge of guiding him around. He also made sure he had lens-cleaning wipes; he'd forgotten those during his first trip, and that had been a hard lesson to learn. Finally, he dug deep until he located his headlamp, and he made sure he had plenty of water and snacks to eat.

The two men climbed out of the SUV and locked it up securely before they set off on a trail that Sam didn't even see until they were on it. He plopped his hat on his head, and they were off, Sam with his camera in his hands and ready for use. He was excited to get some shots of the wildlife here, and he had been waiting for this day for a very long time.

Initially, they hiked the trail without conversation. While it would be a while until they got to the precise spot he wanted to go, he didn't want to scare off any of the wildlife that may give him ample opportunity for a good shot. He kept his eyes and ears peeled, but he didn't see anything in the beginning. He could, however, hear an abundance of living things, their sounds filling the air around him.

His first chance came about thirty minutes in. A Golden Lion Tamarin, a monkey with a beautiful mane, was on a tree branch enjoying its meal. Sam was able to get some beautiful shots of it as it chewed and looked directly at him. He also got some impressive shots of a couple of sloths and a macaw. The rest of the hike was pretty uneventful, and soon the two men arrived at a clearing, where they stopped and set up their site for the day.

Rico had brought a pair of umbrella chairs, which he unfolded and situated while Sam got his essentials out of his pack. He set up his tripod and got his camera ready, then the two men sat to relax for a bit.

"Good shots here for you," Rico said. "Why have you never taken pictures of animals before?"

Sam pulled a granola bar out his pack and opened it. He offered one to Rico, who held his hand up in refusal. "I guess I just wanted to feel my way, you know?" Rico shook his head, so Sam continued. "I wanted to be sure I would do a good job here with plants and people before I tried animals." Rico acknowledged him with a nod.

He was hoping to get some pictures of a jaguar, maybe hunting its prey, or maybe even a couple of the beautiful reptiles that were native to those parts, but he knew not to rush things. Plants didn't move, and people gave permission, but with animals, you had to adjust to their way of doing things, and he knew this. His grandmother had taught him that lesson early on, and it was something he not only practiced but respected. He would be as patient as was needed. He paced a bit, but mostly stood by his camera and kept his ears and eyes opened.

The day seemed to pass all too quickly, though, and the only shots that Sam really got were of a poison dart frog, a kinkajou, and a lizard hopping across the waters of a nearby river outlet. The sun was beginning to sink in the sky, so Sam reviewed his shots, even sharing them with Rico for a second opinion. They were beautiful, and they would do, but he sure hoped that he got some that were more desirable by the next day, maybe big cats or even a toucan.

The two men gathered their things and began hiking back to the SUV, Rico in the front with his large light illuminating the path. Neither of them wanted to be walking around once the sun went down completely; it was simply too dangerous. They would return the next day for more shots.

"I think we will visit another spot tomorrow," Rico was saying. "I found it by accident last year, and lots of animals there for you to take pictures of."

"Sounds good to me," Sam replied. "How far is it from here?"

Rico was panting a bit and had to catch his breath before replying. "Oh, forty minutes I think. A lot of monkey and bird farther up. Maybe even a big cat."

"That would be awesome, Rico. Just what I was hoping for," Sam said.

The men came off the trail right at the car, which Rico unlocked immediately. They put their things inside and climbed into their seats, and Rico started the engine and turned around in the direction they came in. The sun was really sinking now, and Rico had the headlights on bright to help him see. Sam was feeling tired, so he leaned his head back against the seat and closed his eyes while they tooled along.

Rico worked for a company called Expedition Amazon. He had worked there since he was old enough to drive, and being a native, coupled with his experience in the business, he was a huge asset to them. They employed many guides, but Sam had no interest in using anyone but Rico, and he made sure to reserve his services ahead of time.

They pulled up to Expedition Amazon and climbed out. Sam gathered his bag and slung it over his shoulder, then turned to Rico. "I can't wait to hit that new spot tomorrow. What time do you want to leave?"

"My wife has to see the doctor for the baby tomorrow," he replied thoughtfully. "I will go with her, then I come here to meet you. How's eleven?"

Sam nodded with a big smile on his face. "I'll be here."

"Good. See you then," Rico said, and he turned to the car to take it to the lot. "Oh, Sam, wait."

Sam stopped and walked back to the man. "What do

you need?"

Rico glanced over his shoulder, then looked behind Sam as if he wanted to make sure no one could hear them. "You carry a weapon, Sam?"

Sam raised his eyebrows. "What kind of weapon? I thought I wasn't supposed to."

Rico put his forefinger up to his lips and leaned toward Sam to speak quietly. "This new spot, it is not visited often." He continued to glance around. "If you have a weapon, you should bring it. Large cat there; other animals, too. If you don't have a weapon, like a gun, I will bring one for you and me both."

Sam watched Rico carefully. "Are we even supposed to be there?"

Rico shook his head. "No, but the best animals are there."

"Okay. I don't have one, so you bring one for me. I know how to use it," he said, and Rico nodded. "See you tomorrow at eleven then."

"Tomorrow at eleven," Rico replied with a smile, and he jumped into the SUV and sped off to the rear of the building.

Sam whistled as he made his way to the small gravel lot where his rental car was parked. He was staying in a hotel, and he was anxious to get there. He would eat a good supper and get plenty of rest. He was also glad they wouldn't start work until eleven because he wanted to pick up some extra snacks and water, and he also needed to get some more lens cleaning wipes.

He reached the car and put his bag in the back seat,

then got behind the wheel and took off for the hotel. He couldn't hide his excitement and sang as he drove down the road. That was why he liked Rico. Even though he was only a guide, he seemed to appreciate Sam's need for the best pictures. He made a mental note to leave Rico a fat wad of bills when he was finished with his services this time around; he earned a big tip.

CHAPTER 2

Sam woke before sunrise and showered and dressed. He sat at the small desk in his room and opened his computer. He would upload his shots from the day before into the computer for extra safekeeping, and it would also give him time to pick out his favorites. Before he sat down and got comfortable, he ordered coffee and fruit for breakfast through room service. Then he got to work.

He picked his camera up first, while his laptop was starting up and began to view the shots he had gotten the day before. Most of them met his standards: they were good and usable. He ended up deleting several that weren't up to par. Then he plugged the camera memory card into the laptop and started the upload process.

A knock on his door signified that his breakfast had arrived. After tipping the bellboy, he closed the door and sat down to eat. The coffee was strong and delicious, and he was glad they had brought him an entire carafe of the black liquid. He was going to be rearing to go after he polished that off, he knew, and the thought made him smile.

With his breakfast gone and his picture upload

complete, Sam turned on the television to get any news he could find. He would leave in an hour and pick up some needed items, and then he would meet Rico, but until then he was going to relax with the remainder of his coffee in front of the boob tube. Had to keep up with the media, after all.

Around nine thirty Sam had had enough television and more than enough coffee, so he turned the unit off and packed his bag. Double-checking all of his equipment as he did so. He then made his way down to the parking lot, where he put his things in the rental car and took off for the local shopping district. He didn't need much, but what he did need he wanted to be sure to have.

The shopping took him a short time to complete, and soon he found himself sitting in the car with nearly an hour to burn. He decided that he would make his way to Expedition Amazon and wait for Rico to show up. He had nothing better to do, and he had purchased a wildlife magazine that he had not yet had the pleasure of looking at, so that would fill his time.

Fifty minutes later he was still flipping through the magazine, and he had lost track of time.

"What are you doing?" came Rico's voice from directly next to his window. "How long have you been sitting here?"

Sam was startled, and he jumped, spilling the magazine on the floor beneath his feet. "Dammit, Rico! You scared the crap out of me!" The guide laughed as if it was the funniest joke he had ever heard.

Now Sam shook his head and laughed along with the man, then he glanced at his watch. "Nearly an hour, I guess," he replied as he got out of the car and opened the trunk to retrieve his pack. "How did the doctor visit go for your wife this morning?"

"Ah, the baby is good, the wife is good, I'm, how you say, nervous mess?" Rico was joking, of course, and he was beaming with pride. "New baby is gonna look just like me; gonna be a boy."

Sam locked the vehicle and slung his bag over his shoulder as he followed Rico to the SUV, which he had already parked in front of the building. "Did the doctors tell you it is a boy?" he asked.

Rico shook his head as the two men climbed into the vehicle. "No, but I know in my heart. It's a boy, and it looks just like me. I make a good, strong baby."

"I believe it, my man," Sam replied.

Rico started the car, and soon they were off. "Tell me more about this new spot where we are going today," Sam said.

"Well, it's not visited very much from people," he said, his eyes fastened on the road as he looked for the spot where he would turn. "I only go there alone, and only one time, but that time there were beautiful jaguars and other animals. Same as you want to take pictures of."

Sam smiled to himself as he watched the scenery. "I'm excited. I have some very specific animals in mind that I would like to shoot. Hope it's a good day for them."

After about forty minutes Rico pulled the SUV onto a dirt road that Sam hadn't even noticed; he obviously knew exactly where he was going, and that pleased Sam to no end. He was beside himself with anticipation. He would be turning these photos into *Planet Geographic* for a piece on animals of the Amazon, and they would bring him a pretty penny. He desperately wanted to get some good shots.

The dirt road they were on was definitely smoother than the one they traveled the day before, but it was a bit harder to see due to the overhang the trees provided. The air cooled, and it was almost as if they were driving at twilight due to the shade. Sam reached around to the back seat and grabbed his bag. He had already gotten the camera ready at the hotel; now all he had to do was get it around his neck, and he wanted to do that as soon as possible in case a great shot presented itself. He donned the camera and then put his hat on his head.

Suddenly Rico slowed the SUV way down, almost to a crawl. Sam looked over at his guide, who had a serious look on his face. He stopped the car and turned off the ignition, then he began to listen closely.

"What's going on, Rico?" Sam asked, but Rico put his finger to his mouth and focused on the sounds around them. Sam continued to watch him patiently.

Suddenly a woman screamed, and it was blood-curdling.

Rico's eyes shot over to Sam, whose own eyes were as wide as saucers. Now the jungle had the rapt attention of both men, and neither spoke a word or made a sound. Sam found that his heart was pounding in his chest.

The woman screamed again, closer this time. "What the heck is that, Rico?"

Rico's finger was still on his lips, and he shook his head. After a moment he said, "It sounds like a girl or lady, but it's not right."

"What do you mean, 'not right'?" He was speaking in a whisper, scared to make any more noise.

Suddenly something flew out of the greenery on the left side of the car, and it did so quickly. It was so fast that it was blurred, and both Sam and Rico nearly jumped out of their skin.

A loud flapping noise seemed to be right over their heads, and for a fraction of a second, the sound confused the men as they tried to identify what they had heard and seen.

A loud thump jerked them both out of the state they were in. There, on the hood of the SUV, sat a massive bird. It drew its wings in and stared at the two men.

"What the heck is that, Rico?" Sam had never seen anything like it. It was huge.

The bird was beautifully colored. It had long, flowing tail feathers that were purple in color, as were its massive wings. Its head and body were a gorgeous light blue, which complemented the purple perfectly. It was beautiful.

That was when Sam noticed a couple of things that terrified him. First, the beak on the bird measured more than half a foot in length, easily, and it appeared to have two fangs connected to the top portion of its beak; they overlapped the bottom. Its wings sported what appeared to be hands, and they were situated on its torso but were connected to the wings themselves. Finally, Sam took notice of its eyes. This bird had the eyes of a human being, and they were light blue in color.

The bird opened its beak and let out another horrible and terrifying scream.

"Damn!" Sam picked up his camera fumbling with it ferociously to take a picture. After a minute he turned to Rico and said, "Rico, what the heck is it?"

But Rico wasn't listening. He was looking the bird in the eye, and the bird was returning his stare. "Rico?"

But Rico didn't respond or move. Sam watched the bird as it moved its head closer to the windshield. It appeared to be enraptured with the tour guide, and the tour guide appeared to be entranced with the bird. Sam watched the exchange, his mouth was wide open.

Suddenly Rico moved. His right hand moved up to open his door. "Stay here," he whispered to Sam without taking his eyes off the beautifully feathered fowl.

He opened the door and stepped out, then shut it again. The bird was following Rico's every move with its eyes. He stopped next to the car and was only about a foot and a half from the animal. A small smile played on his lips, but only for a second.

The bird opened its massive wings in a move that was so fast it was almost invisible to the naked eye. The hands that were attached to its wings shot out, and the bird sank its nails into Rico's throat, then the needle-like beak drove into first his left eye, then his right, blinding him.

Rico screamed, and for the first time he began to struggle, but the bird had a firm grip on him. Just as sudden as it had landed, it shot into the air, carrying the tour guide with it. It flew until it was out of sight.

Sam thought he was screaming, but after a moment he realized that no sound was coming out of his mouth. He looked down at his hands and realized that he had been shooting pictures the whole time, but the camera was in his lap, his finger pressing the button in a panic. He sat forward and looked to the sky, but there was nothing but treetops.

Sam rolled his window down about half an inch. "Rico!" he screamed, over and over, but he got nothing but silence in return. He began to look frantically at the jungle around him, but all he could see were the plants and trees, and he couldn't hear any of the animals at all. The jungle was eerily still.

Now he realized that he was holding his breath, and he let it out with a whoosh. He was shaking violently, and he thought he was going to be sick, so he took slow breaths to counteract nausea. After a couple of minutes, it seemed to subside, and he was able to begin to pull himself together.

"What the heck?" he asked himself out loud. He had never seen a bird like that in his life, and he had certainly never been taught about such a creature in school. He shook his head as if to clear the picture of the unknown fowl from his mind, but the picture remained, vivid and violent.

"Rico!" Sam called for the guide a few more times, but he knew as surely as he knew his own name that Rico was not going to respond. Finally, he climbed over to the driver's seat, careful to keep his eyes on his surroundings. He turned the key in the ignition, and the engine fired immediately. It seemed deafening in comparison to the loud silence that the jungle was offering.

He turned the SUV around frantically and drove the vehicle back the way it came. He sped as fast as he could without losing control of the vehicle, though a couple of times he was sure he was going to. He had to get back to Expedition Amazon and get some help. All he could focus on was the road before him and the pounding of his heart.

CHAPTER 3

"So, what you are telling me is that one of our tour guides was snatched up by some strange bird?" The director of Expedition Amazon was standing with his rear against his desk, and his arms crossed over his chest. Sam sat before him in an office chair, sweat pouring off of him and tears in his eyes.

"That is exactly what I'm telling you," he replied. "I left my camera in the vehicle. If you just let me get it, I can see if any of the shots I took of the thing came out."

The man, Miguel Pereira, looked incredulously at Sam. It seemed he was suspicious of everything he had just been told. Finally, after studying him for a moment, Pereira said, "Okay, fine. Let us go get your camera."

The two men went out to the vehicle, and Sam grabbed his bag from the back seat and his camera from the passenger seat in the front. He began to view the shots he had taken. It showed he had gotten more than thirty, all but two of them showed blurry views of his lap, shoes, and the floorboard of the SUV.

As soon as he found the first shot of the bird, he began to shake again. "Here. Here it is." He handed the camera over to Pereira and put his hand over his mouth to keep from crying out at the memories of Rico being carried away in the sky.

Pereira looked at the shot, and a look of horror came over his face. "Oh my gosh!" he said under his breath. "What is it?"

Sam could give only a frustrated chuckle and a shrug before finally replying, "I was hoping you could tell me that."

Miguel continued to stare at the picture, horrified, and shook his head. "I do not know. I have never seen anything like this in my life."

Now Sam began to pace a bit, shock still coursing through his veins. "I think we should be trying to go find Rico. We have to save Rico."

Miguel continued to shake his head in disbelief. Finally, he said, "Okay, okay. I am going to call the authorities, and I will put together a group to search for him, but if what you told me is true we will likely not find him alive."

The man handed the camera back to Sam. "I will need you to stay for a while. The authorities will want to speak to you, I am sure. Then I will need you to take the group and me back to where this happened."

Sam's eyes glanced over at the SUV, and for the first time, he noticed a splash of blood across the surface of the vehicle's hood. He closed his eyes tightly to keep from remembering Rico's attack, but it did little to help him. He turned to Pereira. "Fine. I will do whatever you need me to do. But dead or alive Rico must be found."

The two men returned to Pereira's office, where he called the police. He then grabbed a clipboard off a nail on the wall. "I will put together a search party, and you will accompany them back to the site, but you will have to wait to leave until the police have come."

They didn't have to wait long. The police arrived rather quickly and took a statement from Sam. They, too, acted as if he was out of his mind until he showed them the two shots he had gotten of the bird. Then they all acted as horrified as Sam felt.

"I have chosen a group of employees to search for Rico, and Mr. Daniels will accompany them back to the location where the incident took place," Pereira said. "Once you are finished with him I will send the group out."

The older of the two officers spoke. "I think the nature of the incident demands police accompaniment. We will follow your group to the site as well, so you should go ahead and alert your people that we will be leaving.

Pereira gave a curt nod and left the room. Sam collapsed into the chair behind him. The younger officer handed back the camera. "We will need to have copies of the photos."

"Sure, sure," Sam replied. "Anything you need; anything at all."

After a few minutes, Pereira came back into the office. "Okay, my people are getting a couple of vehicles for the search. You will want to take your own, I presume?"

The older officer gave the nod. "We will need to see the vehicle that was being used by this man and the victim."

"It's out front," Pereira replied. "Here are the keys."

Within a half-hour, Sam was sitting in the passenger side of another SUV with three other men. Another SUV followed, and the police were in the rear. At first, Sam had worried he would not be able to get them back to the site, but he soon discovered he could never forget the route. He took them to the spot almost effortlessly.

Rico's blood was on the ground drying. The foliage that covered the road they were on cast great shadows over it. Some of the men started to get out of the vehicles, but Sam sat right where he was. He turned to Pereira, who was driving. "I think I'm going to stay right where I am."

Pereira nodded. "I can understand. I will take you back to our headquarters and let these men begin the search if you wish."

"I wish," Sam said. "Please."

∞

Sam sat straight up in his bed at the hotel. He was panting and gasping and covered with sweat, and it took him a moment to realize he was safe. When he did, he began to shake.

He had dreamed of Rico being carried off by the bird. As it soared through the sky with its nails gouged into his throat, Rico was screaming at Sam, "Help me! Help me!" Blood rained down on the ground below as he disappeared into the distant sky.

Sam wondered if he would ever get a good night's sleep again.

He swung his feet to the floor and padded to the bathroom for a cold drink of water. He downed two glasses and started back for the bed, but when he looked at it a feeling of dread came over him. He would not be getting any more sleep that night. Instead, he would turn on the TV to distract him with its noise and pictures.

By the time the sun rose Sam had showered and packed all of his belongings. He had ordered breakfast from room service but was unable to touch the food. The eggs and sausages sat cold on the plate, staring up at him. He just couldn't eat, not now.

The phone in his hotel room rang obnoxiously at nine forty-five, making him jump. He didn't want to talk to anyone; as a matter of fact, he was cutting his entire trip short to put yesterday's events behind him. He had already contacted the front desk to make them aware of his intentions, so he didn't know who would be calling him. He picked up the receiver with trepidation.

"Hello?"

A man's voice answered him. "Hello. Is this Samuel Daniels?"

"It is," Sam replied.

"Mr. Daniels, this is Miguel Pereira from Expedition Amazon," the man said. "I am calling to let you know that the search party was able to locate Rico Alves."

Sam's eyes lit up. "You did? Is he okay?"

Pereira cleared his throat and said quietly, "No. He

is deceased."

Sam sat down on the bed, the telephone receiver still at his ear. He knew that no one could survive the attack he had witnessed. He had hoped it had been in his head, as his dreams, but it was not.

"He was torn limb from limb," Pereira continued. "His eyes were gouged out, and his abdomen was ripped wide open. We were only able to identify him by his face. The rest of his body was unrecognizable as human. His family has been contacted."

Sam took a deep breath. "Is there going to be a search to locate the bird?"

"My men are preparing to go out and do just that," Pereira stated, "which brings me to the next reason for my call. I will need a copy of the photos you have, and the police need one too. I told them I would ask you to email them to me, and in turn, I would provide them with copies as well."

Sam stood. "Yes, yes. Give me your information, and I will send them to you right now."

Once he had Pereira's email address, he opened his laptop and sent both photos, which he had already uploaded to his laptop. He added a short note asking that the man give Rico's family his condolences, then he sent it on its way. Finally, he gathered his bags and looked around the room one last time before he checked out for good.

The drive to the airport was uneventful, though it seemed to take forever for him to get there and put this trip behind him. He was still in a bit of shock, and he couldn't seem to shake it. Once he turned his rental car in and made his way to his assigned concourse, he was more than eager to go, but he had a couple hours to wait before he would board his flight.

He continued to dwell on yesterday's events. He felt so helpless, so powerless. Was there anything he could do to rectify the situation? He thought not. After all, a man had died.

During his flight home, he made a firm decision: he was going to find out what that bird was, and he was going to return to Manaus. Yes, he would return to Manaus and kill that forsaken creature if it was the last thing he ever did.

R.W.K. Clark

CHAPTER 4

Dr. Katherine Beck strolled down the aisle of her laboratory jotting down notes on a piece of paper on her clipboard. The aisle was flanked with caged animals on either side. Some housed birds, some monkeys, and some mice or rats. The animals squawked and hissed and scrambled around, trying to get her attention.

Technically Kate was an ornithologist, or at least that had been her specialty field of study. Because she was head of the zoology department, she led most of the studies, even though they involved a large variety of animals. Some of the specimens she had in this study were birds, such as a cockatiel and a pair of lovebirds, but working with a wide variety of animals was par for the course when it came to her job. She loved them all, of course, but she particularly enjoyed the occasions when she was able to work with birds and only birds. This study was not one of those occasions, however.

"Oh, you silly babies!" she said and smiled. She was stopping at each and every cage and checking the amount of food eaten, as well as the amount the animals had defecated. "You know I love you, so quiet down."

"Kate, the delivery truck is here." The man's voice

came from behind her, and she turned to see her assistant, Jason Seward. Jason helped her with lab testing and was in charge of cleaning the cages regularly. He had graduated from college last year, so he was fresh and dependable, a bit goofy.

"Thanks, Jason," she replied and motioned for him to come to her. "Here, finish recording their intake and output for me, will you? I'll go sign for the delivery."

She had been conducting experiments for the University of Washington which were centered on animal feed. The study was for a company that made the feed; they had recently changed all of their recipes, making the feed tastier and more nourishing for the animals, and she was in charge of making sure it lived up to their claims before it was put on the market.

Jason took over where she left off, and she made her way to the main entrance of the building. Her regular delivery man stood there smiling at her. He had a crush on her, and she knew it, but he was far too old to even be considered, not to mention that she was way too busy to begin dating.

"Good morning, Rob," she said with a smile. "Did you bring me, my new babies?"

He grinned at her, his eyes filled with admiration. "I'm not sure what babies you are talking about, Dr. Beck, but the box is sure making a lot of noise."

He handed her his 'signature box' as she called it, and she signed it with flair. "Two spider monkeys," she replied. "At least, I hope that's what's in there."

Kate took the package, complete with air holes,

from the delivery man. "Thanks, Rob. I'm also expecting an order of small cages in the next couple of days, so I'll see you soon."

She began to turn away when Rob said, "So, have you thought about my dinner invitation?"

Kate turned back to him. "You know I appreciated it, but I almost live here. Dinner dates aren't something I get to indulge in but thank you. Drive safely, okay Rob?"

She quickly turned around and walked away before he could continue. She hated having to shoot men down, especially if they were good-looking, but the fact was that she really was far too busy for any kind of social life.

Kate made it back to her lab with her package in tow. Jason was at the end of the aisle making notes when she walked in. "Are those the new monkeys?"

"I haven't looked at them yet, but it'd better be," she replied. The last two animal shipments they had received had been completely wrong. One that was supposed to be a pair of guinea pigs ended up being a couple of tarantula spiders, which she didn't need at all. The second one was supposed to be cats, and it ended up being four mice, and one was pregnant.

She put the box on one of the lab tables and donned a pair of thick protective gloves. She loved each and every one of the lab animals, but you never know when one would decide to bite, and those in the box were just going to meet her for the first time. They would be nervous.

Kate cautiously opened the box, all the while speaking in calm, soothing tones. Yes, these were her spider monkeys. A broad grin covered her face. "How are my babies? Nice to meet you, my sweet little babies!"

"I have two cages ready over here," Jason said as she lifted the first monkey out of the box.

She turned to him. "Well, I'm going to need you over here, of course." Jason approached, and when he got to the box, he got in position to close the lid as soon as she had the first one completely out. The little guy screeched and squealed, even as Kate spoke softly.

She crossed the room and put the first monkey in one of the clean, prepared cages. "This is going to be your home for a while, monkey man."

She secured the cage and opened the door to the next one for Jason, who was already carrying monkey number two. In no time they had the monkeys caged up and ready to go.

"Okay," Kate began. "Where is the clipboard? I need to get a monitoring sheet filled out for these two and get some food in their cages."

Jason removed the gloves he was wearing. "Already done, and they're in the proper order with the others. Looks like we're ready to go."

Suddenly the intercom next to the lab door crackled loudly. "Dr. Beck, there is a gentleman here to see you."

"Who is it?" she asked. "I don't have any appointments booked for today. Tell him to make an appointment."

"He says it's an emergency, Dr. Beck."

Kate knit her brow and looked at Jason, giving him an eye roll. "Fine. I'll be out momentarily."

She removed her own gloves and turned to Jason. "I guess I will leave the first feeding up to you. Make sure you document everything, and I'll be back shortly. Whatever happened to people making appointments, anyway?"

Jason smiled. "Everybody loves you, Kate. You're in such high demand."

She snorted sarcastically. "Yeah, right."

The fact was that even though Kate was quite beautiful, she had zero time for socializing or dating. Her parents were convinced that she would die an old maid, thanks to her career. Her mother often told her that her long mane of black hair and piercing green eyes were a waste since she never used them. Ninety percent of the time she had her hair twisted in a bun and ran around makeup-free. The love of her life would likely turn out to be a scientist like herself.

"Okay, Jason, here I go. See you in a few minutes." She left the lab and made her way down the long corridor to the reception desk. She was going to have to remind Martha, the receptionist, that unless visitors had a scheduled appointment, she was not to be interrupted. She had told her several times before, but it seemed that the older woman had a habit of forgetting things often.

When she entered the reception area through the heavy oak door, she found Martha on her computer and a nervous wreck of a man pacing around the room. He carried a large satchel-like bag on his shoulder, and he looked as if he hadn't slept in some time. She noticed how attractive he was, though, with his brown wavy hair and big brown eyes. She shook the thoughts from her mind. She didn't have time to gawk at the male of the species, but she was a woman, after all.

Kate touched Martha's shoulder. "Could I have a quick word with you, Martha?"

The woman gave a tight-lipped smile and rose from her desk. Kate merely took her back through the oak door. "Martha, I've told you time and again that I am not to be interrupted. I consult by appointment only."

"I know, Dr. Beck, and I tried to get him to schedule one and come back, but he refused to leave."

Kate groaned. "Very well, but try to be more assertive in the future please."

The women returned to the reception area, and the man turned to them. Kate extended her hand as she approached him. "I'm Dr. Beck," she said. "Martha tells me you have an emergency. How can I help you?"

The man looked to be a total wreck, with large bags under his eyes, and he trembled slightly as he shook her hand. His eyes even shifted back and forth. "Hi, Dr. Beck. I'm Sam Daniels. Is there somewhere we could talk alone?"

Kate instantly got the impression that whatever the reason for the man's visit, he indeed believed it to be an emergency. Her gut told her she needed to talk to him right away. "Sure, Mr. Daniels. Follow me."

They went through the oak door, and Kate led him

past the lab area to a door at the end of the corridor. She opened it and led him inside; it was her office, and it was the most private area she had available. The room was overflowing with clutter: paperwork, file folders, and books. She grabbed a stack of file folders from a chair and plopped them down on the only empty space she could find on her desk. She turned to Sam, who was looking around the messy space in wonder. "You can have a seat if you like."

Sam gave her a nod and sat in the chair while Kate cleaned off her own chair. After a moment she too took a seat. "What can I help you with, Mr. Daniels?"

Sam let out a huge sigh and shook his head. "I'm not sure how to begin. I was told you are a bird scientist."

"An ornithologist, but zoology, in general, is what I study and practice," she replied.

"Good, good." Now Sam unzipped his bag and took a fancy camera from inside. He stared at the camera in his hands with a grimace on his face, as if he expected it to bite him at any time.

"I'm a photographer, Dr. Beck," he began. "Primarily I photograph plants, wildlife, and the occasional human, but only for magazines like *Planet Geographic* and such."

While Kate was trying to give him her full attention she found herself thinking of her spider monkeys. If this wasn't a true emergency, she was going to give this guy a good chewing-out. She didn't have time for games, and it looked like he wanted to take her picture.

"Last week I flew to Brazil, specifically the Amazon," Sam continued. "First I got some jungle shots, and then I got some pictures of the natives who live there. On the last two days, I spent there, my guide took me back into the jungle for some wildlife shots."

He seemed to grow even more fidgety then, and Kate was getting a bit impatient. He had stopped talking altogether and was staring at his camera once again. She controlled the frustration in her voice.

"Mr. Daniels, I am really very busy. If you have something to ask we really should get down to it."

His head jerked up then, and he looked her in the eye. He appeared to be holding back tears. "I know you are not going to believe me, but I have pictures."

"Pictures of what?"

He cleared his throat and let the camera rest in his lap. "I had a guide named Rico. He was my favorite guide. On the second to last day there, he and I went to a fairly popular area for wildlife, and I was able to get some very good, if not basic, shots of some of the animals there. Nothing out of the ordinary or special."

He paused once again, and Kate squirmed in her chair. "The next day Rico wanted to take me to a spot that was a bit further in, and he was secretive about it. I trusted him, and he said I would get some super shots, so I agreed. We met at the tour office the next morning and headed out.

"We were traveling fairly well when all of a sudden a woman screamed."

Kate was a bit confused, but he had her attention

now. A screaming woman? What did this have to do with birds or animals?

Finally, Sam looked her in the eye, his own face filled with disbelief and fright. "We pulled over and shut off the car, so we could listen. If someone needed help, we were there, but we had to listen.

"We heard it again, but then this… bird, I think… landed on the hood of the car."

Kate noticed that the man was trembling in earnest, now, and beads of sweat were breaking out on his forehead.

"Go on, Mr. Daniels."

He nodded and gave her a superficial half-smile. "I have never seen this sort of bird in my life, and it killed Rico and carried him away."

Now Kate's eyes grew wide. "What do you mean, you have never seen that sort of bird? It's species?"

"I have never seen anything like it. I don't know…" his voice trailed off.

She watched him for only a moment. "I assume you have photographs?"

He nodded frantically and turned his camera on. Kate stood and made her way around the desk toward him. No sooner had she positioned herself behind his chair than the first photo came on. From where Kate was standing it looked to be a large ball of nothing but color initially. Then Sam handed the camera over his shoulder to her.

She took hold of it, glancing at him to see his face had gone ashen. Whatever he was talking about had him scared sick. "Are you okay?" she asked.

He nodded, and Kate focused her attention on the camera screen. What she saw, her mind could not wrap around. If she had to categorize the animal, she certainly would have called it a bird. It was covered in beautiful purple and powder-blue feathers; it was actually quite beautiful and striking. But this thing had a long narrow beak with what appeared to be fangs protruding from it, but that wasn't the most disturbing thing. Connected to its wings, right in the breast area, were what appeared to be five bony phalanges, each tipped with what could only be described as fingernails.

It had human eyes, the color of the sea.

"What the heck?"

Sam gave a hearty laugh. "I know, right?"

She continued to look at the photograph, a feeling of fear and apprehension filling her stomach. She needed to sit down, so she walked to her desk and dropped into her chair.

Kate didn't speak for a few minutes. She was trying to piece the thing together in her mind. It looked nothing like any bird she had ever seen in her life, and she couldn't grasp it. This thing had hands and teeth.

"You are telling me that this… bird… killed your guide?" Kate heard the incredulity in her voice, but her heart was pounding hard. "Tell me everything, but first I would like to upload the photo so I can blow it up and get a better look."

Sam nodded and opened his camera and pulled out the camera memory card. He handed it to her and began relating his horrifying tale as she set about the upload. His voice trembled as he spoke.

"We had stopped the car," he began. "It landed on the hood, hard. My driver was looking at it close, and it was looking right back at him. He stopped talking and became very… preoccupied… with it. It was like the bird was… hypnotizing him with its eyes."

Sam had Kate's full attention now. "What happened next?"

"Well, Rico got out of the car," he continued. "He wanted me to be quiet, so I set about trying to get some shots of the thing. He went up to the side of the car, right at the hood, where the thing was sitting. They kept staring at each other, then… then…"

"Then what?" she asked. "What happened?"

Tears began to fill Sam's eyes, and he shook harder than ever. "I took a couple of pictures, and that was when it happened; it grabbed him by the throat with those hand things." He shook his head and closed his eyes tightly as if to shut out the memory. "Those nail things on the hands sank right into his neck, and then it pecked out his eyes and flew away with him, into the sky. The thing just… flew away… with Rico."

Kate was horrified. She turned her attention back to her computer and printed the photo off. The printer began to make all kinds of noise as it provided the hard copy she had been looking for. She turned back to Sam.

"Can I get you a glass of water or anything?" He only shook his head and wiped at his eyes with his forearm. The printer stopped, and Kate stood up to fetch the picture. She grabbed it and went back to her desk, her eyes fixed on the creature in the photograph.

It was as if she were instantly disconnected from reality. Not only had she never seen such a bird in her life or career, but she had also never seen any fowl remotely like it. Its colors, light blue, and rich purple were captivating, as were its eyes, which seemed to be more a combination of colors rather than any one color at all, and they looked human. Its beak sported treacherous-looking fangs that seemed altogether out of place to Kate, but more than that were the hand-like growths which protruded from its breast area, near the top of the wings.

Kate realized that not only had she stopped breathing, she was also gripping the paper in her fists. After another minute of not being able to pull her eyes away from the thing she forced herself to put the paper-face down on her desk, and even then she struggled to refocus her attention. Finally, she tore her eyes away and looked at Sam Daniels.

He was staring at her intently, his right leg bouncing up and down at a blurring pace. "Well?" he said. "What is it? Tell me you know what it is and I simply have never heard of it or seen it before."

Kate shook her head, her eyes wide. "I have no idea…" she replied, her voice trailing off. "I'm at a loss."

The two sat in silence for several moments, both of them staring at the back of the printed photo sitting on Kate's desk. Her mind was going a thousand miles an hour as it shuffled through the memory files in her brain. Could it be…? No, it would have been discovered long before now. How about…? No, if it were related to that species, it would be extinct, just like them. There was nothing in her accumulation of education and knowledge which could identify the creature in the photo, or even explain it.

"Mr. Daniels, I would like to keep this photo if that's okay with you," she said finally. "I am going to do a bit of research and confer with some of my associates. To be completely honest I can't give you any answers today, but I will get in touch with you as soon as I can. I'm sure this can be explained… somehow."

Sam nodded vigorously. "Yes, yes," he replied. "Keep the picture." He began to rummage through his bag and soon withdrew a small card. "Here is my number and email. I will be eagerly waiting to hear from you; if this is a completely unidentified species, I want to find it. I want to know about it, and I believe the rest of the world will too, considering its seeming penchant for violence."

Sam stood up then and offered his hand to Kate, who stood and accepted the shake. "Let me walk you out," she offered.

The two left her office, both of their minds going in circles. "As I mentioned, I am at a loss, but I do have colleagues with far more experience than I." Kate stopped and put her hand on Sam's arm, causing him to pause as well. Even in his dazed and confused state, he felt the electricity coming from her fingertips. His stomach did a flip-flop, and he felt very shy all of a sudden.

Kate felt it too, and it prompted her to take her hand off his arm quickly. She even blushed a bit, and both of them looked nervously around. "Mr. Daniels," Kate continued. "If this is a new species of some kind it is going to have to be pursued and studied, especially after taking into consideration what happened to your guide during your expedition. I am sure you will want to be a part of that, professionally speaking of course."

"Absolutely!" Sam shifted his weight from one foot to the other and crossed his arms over his chest. "Like I said, I am eager, but not only to photograph the specimen. More than that I want to save lives, and this thing has 'predator' written all over it."

They walked to the main entrance, and after shaking hands once more, the two parted ways. Kate made a beeline for the animal lab where her assistant would be. She was anxious to bounce the information off Jason, if for no other reason than the shock value, but she valued any theories or ideas he could give her; it was why she hired him, after all.

The lab was empty, but Jason's office, located at the very rear of the large room, was open and lit. Kate walked through, chattering at the animals in the cages as she passed them. She approached Jason's open door and rapped on it a couple of times to get his attention.

"Can I come in?" Jason looked up at Kate from his computer, where he had been entering data on the latest tests and on the new arrivals.

He smiled at her. "Sure, Kate. I can't believe you even asked." Jason noticed then that she seemed a bit detached as she made her way, jerkily, to the chair opposite the desk. "Are you okay?"

Kate took note of the concern on his face and in his voice. She attempted to smile at him to reassure him that she was fine, but even she knew she wasn't fooling him. Her smile felt perfunctory and phony.

"Yeah," she said. "I'm okay. I just wanted to talk to you about that visit I just had."

He turned all of his attention to her. "Of course. What's up?"

She thought for a moment, trying to choose her words wisely. Finally, she shook her head in exasperation and let out a sigh. "I think we should go to my office. Words are a bit hard to use in this situation. Are you too busy right now?"

"No, I'm not. I'm actually ahead of schedule." Jason stood and put his white jacket on. "Let's go."

The two walked to Kate's office rather quickly, and she continued to struggle to communicate the entire way. "I'm not even sure how to begin or how to present this to you, so you are going to be a practice round. I'm going to have to present this to other ornithologists, and I have no idea what the best way is." She was rambling, and she knew it, talking more to herself than to him.

"Let's just go a step at a time, Kate." They arrived at her office, and Jason opened the door and held it ajar so Kate could enter first.

The two sat down, and Kate rested her elbows on

her desk and her chin on her hands. She looked over at Jason contemplatively. She was excited, stunned, and in shock. She knew this thing could be big.

"I have something you need to see, Jason."

CHAPTER 5

Sam parked his car in the lot outside his apartment. It was a drizzly day, the sky slate gray and the world damp and weary. He should be used to it by now; after all, this was Washington State.

He climbed from his car and got his bag out of the back seat before pressing the door lock on his key fob. The car gave a 'beep!', and Sam headed inside. He needed some time to study the pictures a bit more himself. He had given it some attention, but the circumstances with Rico's death had interfered with his ability to concentrate effectively. He knew it was time to snap out of it and get into the swing of things.

He unlocked his door and entered his apartment, closing it up behind him. Then he went to the refrigerator and took out a glass bottle of beer and twisted the top off. Putting it to his lips he began to drink, and he nearly downed the entire contents in one gulp. The carbonation hurt his throat, but he felt refreshed nonetheless.

He went into his office at the end of the hall and booted up his computer. He sat down and patiently waited for it to do its thing, then he got into his picture file and pulled up the two photos of the bird. One was a bit blurry, but you could tell what the subject was. The other photo was the one he had shown Dr. Beck, and it was eerily clear. He enlarged it.

It was all Sam could do to keep from staring at the animal on the screen. Its eyes were very, very intelligent, as if it not only knew him, but knew why he was there, and it didn't seem to like it very much at all. It looked almost… angry.

Sam grabbed a rag and damped it with a bit of glass cleaner from the bottom drawer of his desk. He cleaned the monitor screen thoroughly; he didn't want to miss anything or misinterpret anything in the shot. He wanted to see as clearly as possible.

Now he minimized the photo and clicked on his search engine icon. He searched using the only things he could think of: purple and blue feathered bird, hands, fangs, large. He struck the enter key and sat back, draining the last of his beer in one swig.

Results came up quickly, and he clicked on the 'Images' option. Sam went through the results slowly, looking at each one. Most of them were birds he had not only heard of but had photographed or seen face-to-face before. He was beginning to get disappointed.

He clicked to the next photo, and that was when he saw it. It was a photo of a prehistoric bird called an 'archaeopteryx,' but it was much smaller. His heart began to pound; it was as close to the bird in the Amazon as he could find, though it differed in many ways. He clicked on the website attributed to the picture and began to read.

The archaeopteryx was only about as big as a crow or raven. Its beak was shorter and appeared to curve on end, but according to the information it did have teeth. Not only that, it had 'hands.' They were attached to the top of the wings, whereas the Amazonian specimen's hands seemed to grow out of the breast and wings simultaneously. The archaeopteryx was classified as an archosaur, which was actually a reptile class.

Sam continued to read the information provided, and as he did, he became more and more convinced that the bird in the photo was a prehistoric cast-off. Everything he read told him that; a bird like that, with the attributes it possessed, simply couldn't be only a fowl. They simply didn't exist, not then, and not now.

It was a breed of dinosaur, a meat-eating dinosaur with feathers.

Sam sat back hard in his chair, and the breath left his body as he tried to wrap his mind around what he was beginning to understand. "Is this even possible?" he asked himself out loud. "Those things are all extinct; it couldn't have survived…"

After a bit, he leaned forward and hit print. He was going to have it in black and white so he could refer to it, or produce it, for anyone who wanted to see it. As it printed off, he went to the kitchen and grabbed another beer.

He needed all the help he could get.

"So, I could tell right away the guy was a nervous wreck," Kate was saying to Jason. "To be honest, I sort of got the impression that he was kind of loopy."

Jason was listening intently to her as she began the story with a bit of trepidation. "I have to say, though, that now I feel just as loopy myself."

"What did he want, Kate?"

She cleared her throat and shifted herself around nervously in her chair. "He was a wildlife photographer. He gets shots for magazines like *Planet Geo*. Once I learned that about him I relaxed."

Now Kate touched the photo, which was still face down on her desk. "He had just gotten back from the Amazon, and it turned out it hadn't been a very good trip for him." Now she slid the paper back and forth on the desk with her fingers, as if dusting the desk with it.

"Anyway, he had this guide who would always accompany him out when he was there," she continued, then she grew quiet as she thought about the story in its entirety. It seemed far too overwhelming for her to tell the story start to finish, so she mentally threw up her hands and looked Jason in the eye.

"To make a long story short, his guide was attacked and carried off by a large bird, and it doesn't seem to be a familiar species at all."

"What?" Jason asked. "Did he get a shot of it?"

Kate nodded a strange, sarcastic smile on her face and a faraway look in her eyes. "Oh, yeah. He got a shot all right." She picked up the printed copy of the photo

Sam gave her and looked at it for a moment before handing it across the desk to Jason.

The assistant took it, looking at Kate all the while. Finally, he looked down at the paper he was holding in his hand, and his eyes grew wide as his skin went pale.

"What the heck is it?" He looked up at Kate in disbelief before looking back down at it again. "I don't know what this is!"

"Exactly," Kate replied softly.

She let Jason take his time with the photo; after all, she knew exactly how he was feeling. Anyone in their field would need a moment or two to process what he was seeing. He sat staring and shaking his head.

At last, he spoke. "This thing killed a man? Did he say what happened?"

"Oh, yeah," Kate replied. "He told me that the creature landed on the hood of the car they were in. They had stopped because they thought they heard a woman screaming."

"A woman screaming in the Amazon?" Jason was getting more confused by the second. Kate wished he had been sitting in on her meeting with Sam Daniels.

"Yep, a woman screaming." Kate stood and began to pace as she spoke. "The bird landed on the hood, and according to Daniels his guide was staring at it, and he seemed to go into some kind of trance. Anyway, he ended up getting out of the car and standing next to the hood; Daniels was trying to get shots. That was when it happened."

Jason looked up from the photo. "What? What

happened?"

Kate stopped in front of her desk and sat on the edge of it slightly, so she was close to Jason. "According to Daniels the bird, or whatever it is, sank its… hands, or whatever, into the man's neck. Then it pecked his eyes out, and then it took off, carrying him with it."

Jason stared at her in disbelief before looking back down at the picture and shaking his head. He said, "How big was it, supposedly?"

"Daniels didn't say, although it must have a large wingspan to carry the weight of a man." She paused and let her eyes flicker to the image on Jason's lap. "They found the guide's body later on."

Jason squared off his shoulders and handed the photo to Kate as if it were a dirty thing. "So he wanted you to identify it?"

She nodded and chuckled slightly. "Yeah, I have no idea. I can tell you this, though: I'm gonna find out."

Jason sat back and crossed his arms. "It reminds me of a prehistoric species I learned about as a kid. It resembled a bird, but science tagged it as more of a lizard, a member of the dinosaur family. It was called an 'archteryx,' or archaeopteryx. Yeah, that's it! Archaeopteryx!"

Kate went around to her side of the desk and jiggled the mouse to her computer. The screen lit up, and she clicked on her search engine. "How do you spell it, do you think?"

"Heck, I don't know," he replied.

"Try 'a-r-c-h-e-c—"

Kate was typing; then her eyes lit up. "Here, I think this is it: archaeopteryx." She spelled it for him as she clicked on the word and pressed enter.

Jason came to her side of the desk, and in a short time, she had several images pulled up of the creature, which was said to have lived as far back as the Mesozoic era. It was thought to be a 'mid-point' species: not quite bird, and not a dinosaur, though more the latter than the former.

Kate sat in her desk chair and held the photo of the specimen up to the screen. "There are some definite differences, but I guess it is a pretty close call."

"I'd have to agree," Jason replied. "You realize that you need to consult with some other doctors. I mean, you're obligated."

Kate nodded thoughtfully. "Yes, but I'm inclined to keep most of the information to ourselves. I mean, let's face it, this could be big. I'll confer, but I'm keeping all the details out of the mix for now. If this is a new find, I want to be involved, as I'm sure you do."

The two continued to stare at the screen for a while longer, then Kate picked up the receiver to her desk phone. "Martha, will you get me Harold Kreiger please?"

R.W.K. Clark

CHAPTER 6

Sam lay on his bed with his eyes closed. He had been awake for about ten minutes, but he was sporting a major hangover. He knew he was still in his clothes, and he had already deduced that he was not only on top of the blankets, but his head was at the foot of the bed as well.

He lay thinking of getting in the shower and making some stiff coffee. He wished he had some of the coffee he'd had in Brazil; he would wake up in no time if he did. That's when he remembered Rico and… the bird.

Sam sat up quickly then and shook his pounding head back and forth, trying to shake out the thoughts of his dead friend. He put his head in his hands and held his breath; he didn't want to think about Rico at all. The whole situation had traumatized Sam beyond words.

Suddenly the phone on his nightstand rang so loudly it seemed almost vicious. He winced painfully and grabbed the receiver. The ringing was cut off right away.

"This is Sam Daniels," he said, his eyes squinting against his headache.

"Mr. Daniels, this is Dr. Beck with the university," the caller began.

Now Sam's eyes flew open, and he was awake. "Yes! Dr. Beck! Good morning."

"Good morning," she replied. He sounded sick or at least hung over. She was willing to bet the latter was true. She'd get drunk too if she had seen what he claimed to have witnessed. "I was calling to let you know that I have set up a meeting for eleven this morning with Dr. Harold Kreiger. He's with our paleontology department here. I thought we should attend together; after all, this was your experience."

"Sure!" Sam stood and tried to unbutton his jeans while holding the receiver to his head with his shoulder. "So, do you want me to meet you at that department a little early?"

Kate thought for a moment. "Actually, I thought we could meet at my office around ten-fifteen. There were a few things I thought we should discuss, some theories and such."

"Fine, fine." Sam fell back onto his mattress, his feet in the air as he tried to free his legs from his jeans. "I'll see you at ten fifteen in your office."

"See you then."

The call was disconnected. Sam looked at the clock on his nightstand: eight thirty. He jogged to the kitchen in his underwear and quickly made a pot of coffee before jumping in the shower. He wouldn't make it anywhere without a load of caffeine.

∞

By nine he was sipping his coffee and putting the articles he had printed off in a manila folder to take with him. He made sure he printed off copies of the good photo of the bird so everyone could have one if needed. He also forced himself to eat an English muffin. Something had to soak up the alcohol he had drunk.

By nine forty-five Sam was on I-5 heading to his meeting with Dr. Beck. The traffic wasn't too bad, though he was making much slower progress than he would have liked. He found himself thinking about Kate Beck as he drove. He recalled her hand on his arm, and his stomach did another flop. Not only was the woman smart, but she was also quite beautiful as well.

He thought about her hair, which was as black as night. She had it pulled back when he was there, with wisps hanging down from her temples. Her eyes! As green as emeralds, and tantalizing.

Sam realized he was smiling like a dope. He reached down and turned the radio on. He would be there soon enough, and the last thing he needed was to swoon like a schoolboy in her presence. This was an important business meeting. There was no time for flirtations and fantasies.

He ended up parking his car outside the zoology department at ten seventeen. He hated being late, so he grabbed his bag and jogged into the building. The receptionist looked up when he came through the door.

"Hello, Mr. Daniels," she greeted him. "Dr. Beck is expecting you. Do you remember the way?"

"Yes, thank you." He looked at the name plaque on her desk. "I'll just go on back, Martha."

She smiled and went back to her tasks. Jason

followed the route which would take him to Kate Beck's office, and soon he found himself knocking at her door.

"Yes?" He heard her voice clearly. "Come in, please."

Sam turned the handle and opened the door enough so she could see it was he. She smiled broadly and stood up with her hand out. "Good morning, Mr. Daniels. I'm glad you came in a bit early. There were some points I thought we should cover before we head over to Dr. Kreiger's office if that's okay with you."

Sam nodded and stood there awkwardly. "Have a seat, please." Kate gestured toward the chair he had used the day before, then she sat at her own desk. "So, after you left, my assistant and I did a bit of research, and we think that the creature in question may actually be prehistoric. Hence the appointment with a paleontologist."

Sam's eyes lit up. "I did some research as well!" he opened his bag and pulled out the manila file. "It looks a lot like an arch… archae…" He was fumbling to find the word amongst the papers.

"Archaeopteryx?" Kate finished for him.

Sam let out a major sigh of relief and blushed at his own verbal fumbling. "Yeah. Thank you."

She smiled and nodded, and he got goosebumps. Wow, was she gorgeous or what? He felt like a dolt in her presence.

"We found the same, but the specimen you photographed seems to have evolved a bit differently unless that is what the archaeopteryx actually looked like and we have been off base for centuries," she said. "Perhaps full grown remains were never discovered?"

Sam laughed nervously, and Kate continued. "With all that being said, my assistant, Jason Seward, will be joining us in the meeting. He is a little better with things of a prehistoric nature."

Now she shifted slightly, and the smile faded from her face. "I don't know how you will feel about this, but I assume that you are interested in figuring this all out, not only for your friend who was killed but also for the recognition you would get for the discovery?"

Sam thought for a moment. "Yes, it is about Rico, but if this is a new and undiscovered species, others need to know."

"You are aware that you would receive credit for the discovery, correct?"

Sam shrugged and stayed quiet.

Kate continued. "I am interested in the discovery for those reasons mostly, and I am more than willing to assist you in whatever needs to be done, but I strongly feel we need to keep the details to ourselves, such as location. In this business, people can be pretty deceiving. You don't want anyone stealing your thunder."

Sam thought about it. "No, of course not."

"So," she said, the smile back on her face. "It will likely be necessary to travel back to the location. Capturing the specimen will be very important if we are to study it at length. My assistant and I are eager to be a part of this with you if that's okay."

Now Sam's mind went right out the door. That meant he would get to travel with this hot little vixen. He would get to know her, and vice versa. Spending time with her was all he was thinking about.

"Absolutely, Dr. Beck," he replied.

Kate stood up, a broad grin on her face. "You may as well call me Kate. I'm going to fetch Jason, and we'll head on over to Dr. Kreiger's office. Be right back."

She left the room and closed the door behind her, leaving Sam to his schoolboy crush thoughts. When he was around her it seemed he could think of nothing else; not the bird, not fame and fortune, not even poor Rico and his pregnant wife. It was the least he could do. Find the bird and get established information, even if he was distracted by a beautiful ornithologist.

He waited there in her office, fidgeting like mad. He went through his bag for no reason. Then he paced and looked at the variety of things she had on a bulletin board, none of which made any sense to him. She had a small compact disc player and a stack of discs, which he went through. They made him smile; she liked heavy metal.

He was just beginning to look at books in a bookshelf, all of which appeared far too advanced for him to understand when Kate and her assistant returned. "Sam Daniels, this is my assistant, Jason Seward. Jason, Sam Daniels."

Jason's eyes lit up, and he offered his hand, which Sam accepted. He had been worried when she told him her assistant was a man, but this guy was just a kid, maybe twenty-two, quite possibly younger. Sam was relieved.

"It's nice to meet you, Jason." The men shook hands, and then Sam stepped back.

Jason said, "How exciting for you, to find this specimen, I mean."

Sam took a deep breath. "I guess in a way. The manner in which it was discovered wasn't all too pleasant, I might add."

Jason's face grew serious. "Of course. I understand. I am sorry about your guide."

Sam nodded thanks, and Kate interjected. "Are we ready, gentlemen? Bring anything with you that you want to share or discuss. Dr. Kreiger will be interested in anything and everything."

She grabbed a file and Sam put his bag on his shoulder. The three of them then left to head over to the paleontology department. As they walked Sam picked up on the electric excitement both Kate and Jason exuded. He assumed something like this was quite exciting for people in their profession.

He was glad he was not alone on this journey. He wouldn't know the steps to take, but Kate made him feel completely comfortable. He was very thankful that she agreed to assist him.

At least he would have the chance to get to know her better if nothing else.

R.W.K. Clark

CHAPTER 7

"So, Katie, what have you got for me today, love?" Dr. Harold Kreiger spoke with a light, teasing humor. He was a short, round man, balding just a bit on top. His light blue eyes were intelligent and playful.

Kate did the introductions, and they all took a seat at a conference table. In the middle of the table was a pitcher of water, a pot of coffee, sugar, cream, stirring sticks, and a stack of cups. Dr. Kreiger encouraged them to help themselves. Then he sat back, his eyes fixed on Kate.

"You really didn't give me much information, so I'll need filling in. You want to see if I can help identify a discovery. That much you told me," Kreiger said. He sat back and waited.

Kate began. "Well, Harold, Sam here is a wildlife photographer. On his last trip, he and his guide encountered what appears to be a bird of unknown origin." She opened her folder and withdrew a copy of the photo, which she handed over to Kreiger. They sat in silence as he picked it up and gave it a look.

Kreiger's face changed dramatically in the next few seconds. His smile faded and his brow knit. He squinted and leaned closer to the photo. When he sat back, he almost looked to be in shock.

He looked at Sam. "You took this picture? When?"

"Last week," Sam replied nervously.

"Where was this at?"

Kate spoke up. Touching Sam's leg as to stop him. "Do you know what it is, Harold? Do you have any theories?"

If Kreiger recognized her diversion, he didn't let on. He looked at Kate and cleared his throat. "To tell you the truth I think it is likely prehistoric in nature, but that's impossible now, isn't it?"

Kate smiled. "All three of us have done a small bit of research, and that was our conclusion as well. Why do you think I called you, Harold?"

Kreiger smiled slightly. "Of course. It certainly wouldn't be on a whim with someone as thorough as you, Kate."

He turned his attention back to the photo, then continued. "It resembles the archaeopteryx, or at least as far as we can tell by fossils of the species that have been found. Obviously, modern science has never actually seen one. The phalange growths are a bit different than those in the fossilized archaeopteryx, however. They seem to be not only connected at the wing tip but at the creature's breast as well."

Sam spoke up. "The hands, or whatever they were, are much larger than the ones on your dinosaur bird, though."

Kreiger nodded. "I have noticed that," he said. He

took a deep breath and continued without looking up from the photo. "They actually look quite massive, to be honest. Did the creature behave calmly, or in a hostile manner?"

Sam laughed out loud then. Dr. Kreiger looked at him in confusion, which prompted Kate to speak. "Mr. Daniels' guide was killed by it."

Kreiger's face looked a bit stricken, almost as if he didn't quite believe what he was hearing, yet trusted the one doing the speaking. "I'm sorry to hear that," he said quietly. "Do you mind if I ask for more details?"

Sam collected himself and looked at Kate, who gave him a single nod and said, "The basics would be fine I think, Sam."

He took a deep breath and began, weighing his words carefully to not divulge too much information. He would hate to slip up, particularly when Kate Beck had been so clear in her office before they came. Sam cleared his throat and shifted in his chair.

"My guide was someone who had been with me on other occasions; he was something of a friend, actually."

Kreiger interrupted. "When you say 'guide' I assume you were on a safari of some sort."

"No," Sam replied slowly, looking Kreiger in the eye. "I was on assignment for work. Anyway, we were driving to a new area, an area he alone seemed to be familiar with. That was when we heard the screaming, and he pulled over and parked the car."

"Screaming?" Kreiger asked.

"It sounded like a woman was screaming in the ju…,

I mean, in the woods." Sam had nearly slipped up, but Kreiger didn't seem to catch it, so he continued. "We pulled over to listen, and that was when the bird, or whatever it is, landed on the hood of the car. My friend was staring at it, and to be honest, it looked like the damn thing was… hypnotizing him or something."

Kreiger nodded and waited for Sam to continue. "He looked spacy, almost like he couldn't look away. I wanted to get some shots, as I had never seen anything like it in my whole career, and that was when he got out of the car and stood next to the hood. He was still looking the thing in the eye. All of a sudden it sank its… fingers, or whatever, deep into his neck, poked his eyes out one at a time with its beak and then flew off with him. Would you please excuse me?"

Sam stood up and left the office to pull himself together. Kreiger looked at Kate and Jason. "I take it you are interested in finding this thing again?"

"You would be correct," Kate replied. "But not for the reasons you may think. They found the body of his guide later; anyone in the area is at risk. The creature needs to be captured and studied."

Kreiger chuckled. "It certainly wouldn't hurt your career to discover a new species either, would it?"

Kate didn't respond, so Kreiger continued. "I would like to be involved if that is at all possible."

"That is something I would have to discuss with Mr. Daniels," she said. "Meeting with you is only the first step. The three of us, and I mean Sam, Jason, and myself, would have to discuss our options in greater detail. Tell me, Harold, why you would want to be involved? What would your motive be?"

"Science, plain and simple," he said.

Kate knew better. Yes, to an extent she could understand him wanting to be involved for science, but as Kreiger himself had said, a discovery like the one they were discussing would mean big business for anyone in science. It would be a game-changer, and they all knew it. But she wasn't about to let anyone snatch this out of her hands, or Sam's for that matter, and that was exactly what would happen. The traumatized photographer would be elbowed out altogether.

She stood up and gestured for Jason to do the same. "I think we can probably close up this conversation." She reached over and picked the photo up from the table in front of Kreiger, who looked just like a child whose mother just took away his favorite toy. "We'll discuss it and get back to you. Thank you for seeing us, Harold."

Now Kreiger stood and walked around the conference table to shake Kate's hand. "It would be beneficial to both you and Mr. Daniels to have someone knowledgeable in paleontology to accompany you and study with you. I'm telling you, Kate, this thing is prehistoric in nature. You are going to have your hands full. After all, you're an ornithologist."

"I'll keep that in mind, Harold." Kate shook his hand, then she and Jason left the room to go find Sam.

Kreiger watched the door close behind them, his arms crossed over his chest. After a moment he walked over to the telephone and picked up the receiver. He punched only a few numbers in before saying, "Roy, it's Harry. Can you come to the conference room? I have something I want to talk to you about. Fine. I'll see you in a bit." He hung up the phone and then sat back down at his place at the head of the conference table.

He steepled his fingers and let his chin rest on them. He felt himself getting all worked up emotionally. All his years of study and hard work, all his dedication to his science, and a bird specialist and photographer walk in with the greatest discovery in the history of the world, since the beginning of mankind. It infuriated him, and he wasn't about to let this opportunity be wasted on people who couldn't possibly give a damn.

He thought of Roy Hastings, the man on the way to see him. He was another paleontologist, and Kreiger was certain he would feel the same way. He would fill him in on what he had learned, and together they would figure out how to snake their way into this thing. It didn't matter to Kreiger what they had to do; he was willing to do anything. Roy Hastings would be too.

Even if they had to lower themselves to thievery, they would be the individuals that would receive recognition for this find; he would see to it.

CHAPTER 8

Jason and Kate stood outside the men's room door at the paleontology department. Sam was in there, and they were waiting for him to come out. After a few more minutes the doorknob turned, and he emerged, his hair damp around the edges from splashing water on his face.

"Sorry," he said sheepishly. "I just needed to have a minute."

Kate smiled. "It's okay, Sam. Anyone in your situation would be a mess. Anyone." The three began to walk out of the building. "I think we should talk in my office. There we can begin to plan our next move." She put her hand on his shoulder. "We have a lot to discuss."

"I'd say," Jason chimed in. "To be honest, I can't see Kreiger giving up this easily; no way."

By the time they reached Kate's office, Sam was ready for the day to be over. He hoped any conversation they had would be brief; he could feel a nasty headache coming on. He sat in the chair across from Kate's desk and looked up at her.

"Can we make this fairly quick? I'm not feeling so

hot," he said.

Kate reached out and put the back of her hand to his forehead. It tingled there, and he found his heart beating faster from her touch. "Sure thing, Sam. How about we say this for now: don't talk to anyone about this, okay?"

Sam nodded, then Kate continued. "We can meet again tomorrow. That will give Jason and me some time to confer and figure out the next best step. I can promise you someone from paleontology, or anyone for that matter will try to contact you. Don't divulge any information."

"I've got it," Sam replied as he stood up. "You know, I may not be a scientist, but I certainly have my own reasons for wanting this. I mean, after all, I've been through enough that I feel I deserve it, and as courteous as that Kreiger was, his attitude left me with a bad taste in my mouth."

Kate nodded, satisfied with his response. "Don't underestimate the lengths he will go to for this to have his name all over it."

"Got it," Sam replied. "Look, I'm gonna head home. I need to rest my head a bit. See you tomorrow?"

"How about nine in the morning?" Kate asked.

Sam gave half a grin. "Perfect. See you two then." With that, he left her office.

Kate sat down at her desk. "Jason, I expect that you are aware that Kreiger isn't going to give up as easily as he'd like us to think. We are going to have to act fast. I say we head to the location with Sam as soon as he can stomach it. What do you think?"

Jason raised his eyebrows. "I think if we put it off we'll regret it. I can almost promise you that Kreiger is scheming as we speak."

Kate nodded and looked out the window. "Let me think on it. I'll formulate the best plan for the situation, and have it ready to present to Sam in the morning."

∞

Roy Hastings and Harold Kreiger had just finished discussing the situation. At first, Roy had been a bit incredulous when Kreiger related the story, but by the time he was filled in he knew with a surety that they had an opportunity of a lifetime fall in their laps.

They would have to tread lightly if they wanted to have this discovery for their own. The first step would be to find out where this Sam Daniels character had been when the bird showed itself, and from the way Kreiger said his visitors had been acting, it was not going to be an easy feat. As a matter of fact, Roy and Harold might have to take some criminal measures to turn the tables in their favor.

"I wish they hadn't taken the damn picture from you," Hastings said toward the end of their conversation.

Kreiger growled a bit. "It doesn't matter. I'm telling you, except for the size of the phalanges and the shape and length of the beak, this thing really could be an archaeopteryx; it is certainly related at the very least."

"What do you want to do about it?" Hastings asked.

"Well," Kreiger replied, "the first thing we have to

do is find out where Daniels was when he discovered it."

"How do you propose we go about that?" Roy quizzed.

Kreiger smiled, and it dripped with deviant motive. "First we'll be nice about it. We'll try to meet up with him alone, so we need to find out where he lives. That will be the first step."

Harold Kreiger was certain that they could infiltrate this entire thing and make it their own, and he didn't care who got hurt in the process.

∞

Sam unlocked the door to his apartment and let himself in. As soon as he closed the door behind him, he leaned against it wearily and gave a big sigh of relief. It was just after noon, and he was already prepared to fully put the day behind him.

After a moment he gathered his wits and locked the apartment door. He put his bag on a chair next to it and made his way into his kitchen. The truth was he wanted another beer, but he wasn't about to put himself in the same situation he was in this morning: hungover and emotional. Nope, he would pass.

He put a Salisbury steak TV dinner in the microwave and started the timer, then went into the living room and turned the television on. The news blared forth, making Sam wince, so he turned it down and then flipped to the channels until he came to a rerun of *Walker: Texas Ranger*. Chuck Norris was always empowering.

The microwave bell dinged, and he went to the kitchen. He took it out and stirred the potatoes, which were still frozen in the middle, then he returned it and set the timer again. His stomach was beginning to rumble, and he was eager to eat.

Just as he started the microwave again his telephone rang.

Sam jumped, startled, and looked at the extension hanging on the kitchen wall. He considered answering but decided against it. He walked up to the phone and looked at the caller ID screen on the back of the receiver. It was a local number, but he didn't recognize it. Nope, no answer this time, telemarketers. After several rings, it stopped, and Sam turned the ringer to the off position.

After a bit his dinner was made, so he grabbed the hot tray from the microwave and took it gingerly to the living room. He put it on the coffee table and went back to the kitchen, where he got a glass of milk, a fork, and a napkin. He would eat, watch a bit of TV, and then take a leisurely nap; that was his plan.

He had just sat down before his meal when the phone rang again, this time from the bedroom. "Grrr," he said. He sat a minute, planning to ignore it again, but he decided to answer it and get it over with. He went back to the kitchen and picked up the phone.

"Hello?" Sam snarled.

"Samuel Daniels?" It was a man's voice, and one he didn't recognize. Damn telemarketers.

"That's right," he replied, his voice less than

pleasant. "To whom am I speaking?"

"Mr. Daniels, this is Dr. Roy Hastings," the man replied. "I'm a paleontologist with the university and an associate of Dr. Kreiger. I understand you met with him today regarding a recent discovery?"

Sam closed his eyes and shook his head. Boy, that Kate was a sharp one. He had barely been home twenty minutes, and the phone started to ring. Jeez.

"Yes, I had a meeting with Kreiger today, but I don't have time to talk with you now."

Hastings cleared his throat. "Mr. Daniels, if you could give me just a minute of your time…"

"Look," Sam said sharply, "Now is not a good time, okay? Thanks, but no thanks."

He slammed the receiver down and then went into his room and shut the ringer off on his bedside phone. Next, he got his cell phone out of his bag in the living room and did the same thing. How the heck had those guys gotten his number already? Then he began to wonder if Kate had not given it to them. He decided to call her and find out. He opened the cell and called her number.

"Hello, Kate Beck," her voice greeted him.

"Um, Kate, this is Sam Daniels," he said. "I'm sorry to bother you. I just got a call from a Dr. Roy Hacket, no, Hastings. Roy Hastings. I've only been home for a little while, and I wondered if you had given it to him."

Kate was still for a moment, then her calm voice said, "Hi, Sam, I hope you're feeling better, and no, I didn't give your number to anyone. Like I said, they aren't going to go away so easily."

"What should I do?" he asked, the frustration he felt obvious in his voice.

Kate sighed, quietly fuming on the other end. "Just don't answer if they call for now. I'll give Kreiger or Hastings a call, probably both."

"Thanks," he said. "I'm going to eat and catch a few zees. I'll see you in the morning."

"See you then," Kate replied, then they disconnected.

Sam went back to his now-cooled TV dinner and groaned. He ate it fairly fast then lay down on the couch with an afghan his mother had made him when he was in college. He was sleeping in only minutes, the television droning hypnotically in the background.

∞

Kate hung up the telephone after speaking with Sam and stood up angrily at her desk. She knew Kreiger was not going to go away easily. She probably shouldn't have gone to him about the bird, or whatever it was. If anyone had an idea of what species it was, it would be he. She was glad that Sam had chosen to call her rather than agreeing to talk to Roy Hastings.

She removed her white lab coat and hung it on a wooden hook next to her office door. She was going to have to show a little muscle to the guys in paleontology. They weren't going to disappear, and if they were as dedicated to their science as she was, she could expect a load of sneaky and conniving behavior on their part. Any muscle she showed would only serve to let them know that she wasn't going to let them trample over her or Sam, but they needed to know that she would take whatever measures were needed to ensure that the discovery stayed in Sam's rightful hands.

She left her office and walked down the corridor to the lab. Jason was inside jotting notes on his trusty clipboard. Kate opened the door and greeted Jason.

"So, how are the kids?" She asked in a very matter of fact tone, with no giddy playfulness in her voice.

Jason recognized the stiffness and abruptly looked up at her from his work. "They're fine. What's wrong with you?"

Kate leaned against one of the lab stations and sneered. "I just got a call from Sam Daniels. He got a call from Roy Hastings over in Kreiger's department."

"Ah," Jason replied as he went back to jotting notes. He finished and clicked his pen closed and put it in his pocket. "We expected something like this, didn't we, Kate?"

"Yes, but I didn't expect them to be so quick to jump on the bandwagon," she said. "I'm going to go over to paleontology and have a strong word with Kreiger."

Jason put the clipboard on his desk and walked to where Kate was standing. "Do you think it will do any good?"

Kate shrugged. "I don't expect it to, but they need to know we are not going to let them at this without a fight. I'm going to make a problem for him he'll never forget if he doesn't lay off."

"Considering that this… bird seems to be extremely 'prehistoric' looking, they likely think you're the one stepping on toes," Jason countered. "Do you want me to go with you?"

"No," she replied as she straightened her posture. "I can handle it. You know, I realize that this find is beneficial to the career of the one involved, but I hope you understand that I want it handled correctly. If this thing is as dangerous as Sam describes then the situation has to be handled with kid gloves, for the safety of everyone. Kreiger would be willing to forego all safety measures just to get his name in print."

"Look, Kate," Jason said, "I know how driven you are, but I also believe you want what's best. Do what you have to do when it comes to Kreiger, but stick to your guns if you are concerned about the ethical aspects of the situation."

Kate smiled and gave Jason a hug. "Since we're really honest here I should probably tell you that I am so excited I can barely breathe."

Jason shook his head and grinned back. "So, is it the bird and only the bird that has your excitement, or is some of it about your new friend Mr. Daniels?"

A blush crept up her cheeks. She gave Jason's left arm a playful punch and said, "You know I don't like to mix business with pleasure."

"Hmmm," he observed. "From the looks, you have been giving him I would be willing to bet that you have considered making an exception to the rule."

Kate made her way to the lab door. "This is about

the discovery, and that's all, Jason. I'm going to go see Kreiger now. If I'm not back in an hour, send help."

With that, she left the lab, a smile on her face in spite of the anger she felt. Okay, so Jason had made a minor point: she did find Sam Daniels to be attractive. Well, maybe more than attractive; he was smoking hot, but this wasn't about her love life.

"Martha," she said as she approached the receptionist. "I'm going to step out for a short while. I need to see Kreiger again. Please make sure I get my messages, okay?"

The older woman flashed a smile. "Sure thing, Dr. Beck."

She stepped out of her building and into the sunlight. She lifted her face to it to soak up as many of the rays as she could. After all, it was Washington; who knew when it would poke its head out from behind the clouds again?

CHAPTER 9

"Well, Roy, I didn't expect him to be so forthcoming right away," Kreiger said to the man seated across the desk. "I'm pretty sure our Dr. Beck has been coaching him. They dodged my questions about location very successfully."

"So what do you propose we do, Harold?" Hastings was seated comfortably, with his legs casually crossed and his hands resting in his lap.

Kreiger stood and began to pace; it always helped him think more clearly if he was moving. "Well, we're certainly not going to give up. I am going to guess that wherever the thing was found, Kate will be taking him there. They will try to secure the discovery soon. She's not one to waste time."

"Should we be watching her?" Hastings asked. "I'm sure she will be the one to make travel plans. The university would pay for them under the circumstances. A simple personal tail will allow us to find out any trips she may plan."

"Good idea," Kreiger said. "We'll want to start right away."

His office intercom crackled as it came to life. "Dr.

Kreiger, Kate Beck is here to see you."

Kreiger raised his eyebrows and looked at Hastings, who also sported a look of genuine surprise. "Send her back, Amelia, and thank you."

"What do you think this is about?" Hastings asked.

Kreiger sat in his desk chair, an amused look on his face. "I would love to think she is coming to tell us she had a change of heart, but she's probably going to chew us out for calling Daniels. Like I said, she's coached him, I'm sure."

There was a strong knock at the door, and before Kreiger could bid her entry, Kate turned the knob and walked in. "Hello, gentlemen. Dr. Hastings, fancy seeing you here!"

Hastings shifted his weight nervously in his chair. He never had been one for confrontation, though Kreiger seemed to thrive on it. He offered her a weak smile instead and turned his attention to his thumbnail.

"What can I do for you, Kate?" Kreiger asked. "Have you come to tell me you've had a change of heart?"

Kate smirked and stood behind the empty chair next to Hastings, her hands gripping its back. "Wouldn't that be nice for you? But I'm sure you know better."

"So what do you need then?"

Kate cleared her throat and held Kreiger's eyes. "I've come to speak with you about how inappropriate and unethical it was for you to enlist Hastings in your plan to discover the location of Daniels' find."

"Why would I do something like that?" He tried to

look genuinely confused, but Kate wasn't buying it.

"You should know, Dr. Kreiger, that our plans are already established for travel," Kate lied. "If you bother Mr. Daniels again I will be reporting you to the school board. I came to you for assistance, not to turn you into an obstacle on our path. As a fellow scientist, I would expect your support and encouragement, not professional larceny."

Kreiger let out a loud belly laugh and leaned forward, putting his elbows on his desk. When his laughter subsided, he looked her square in the eye. "Kate, you know I would never step on a fellow scientist's toes. I only thought that we could be a great help, especially with this… things… origin. You would have to agree that it is much more up my alley than yours."

Kate was disgusted that she had ever trusted Kreiger, and she was even more surprised at how easily lies rolled off his lips. She shook her head and continued. "Were you not so overbearing and rudely persistent you would have had a far better chance at worming your way in."

The room fell into an awkward silence before Kreiger said, "Fine, Kate. If you are this insistent I'll let it be, and I'll even do you one better: I wish you and Mr. Daniels the best of luck."

Kate studied his face, and though he appeared genuine, his eyes gave him away. "Thank you, Harold," she said simply, then she turned on her heel and abruptly left the office.

Kreiger stood and crossed the room to the door. He opened it and peeked out to see Kate striding down the corridor to leave. He shut the door and turned back to Hastings. "Yes, Roy. Check the airlines and see if any tickets have been purchased on the university's account. If not, keep checking." He sat back at his desk. "I think we should send in a dummy, you know, someone to 'befriend' our Sam Daniels. Make it simple."

Hastings stood up and adjusted his slacks. "Sure thing. I actually have a couple of ideas already. I'll be in touch."

Roy Hastings left Kreiger's office. Kreiger sat at his desk staring at the door and thinking. He was going to find out where this creature had been discovered if it was the last thing he ever did.

∞

Sam woke startled. At first, he was confused about where he was, but in only a moment he remembered lying down on his sofa. He glanced at his watch and saw that it was just six in the evening, so he sat up and stretched out a bit before padding into the kitchen.

He opened the refrigerator and saw a taco box with a couple of hard shells he had saved. He fished them out and stood at the counter eating them, then he washed them down with milk. Sam gave a healthy belch and went back to the living room.

He remembered then that he had turned his phones all off. He saw his cell on the end table by the couch, so he grabbed it and looked at the screen: no missed calls. Next, he turned on both house phones before returning to the couch and lying back down.

His headache was gone, so he turned the volume up slightly on the television. The channel was showing some kind of reality show with people bidding on storage units. He didn't have any desire to watch such rubbish, so he turned to the *Planet Geographic* channel and settled in.

Sam found himself remembering the call he had received from that university guy earlier, and he shook his head at the recollection. Kate had been right. He believed he was going to have to be very careful indeed. He didn't want to ruin anything.

Kate. Her face floated behind his closed eyes, and it made him smile. He had been so busy with his career he hadn't had time to work on a personal relationship of any kind. As a matter of fact, he didn't even think about it. Then, all of a sudden, there was Kate Beck, and he found himself wondering if she thought about him. He found himself actually thinking about becoming 'involved.' It could be perfect with a professional like himself. They would both be working on their careers, and neither would feel let down because of the work of the other. He hoped that he would get to know her better, and this 'bird,' or whatever it was, was the ideal icebreaker.

He fell asleep a short time later, Kate Beck filling his dreams.

R.W.K. Clark

CHAPTER 10

Kate Beck let herself into the main door of her department earlier than usual. It was five thirty in the morning, and her meeting with Sam wasn't until nine, but she wanted to spend some time with the animals, her 'babies.' Things had been so hectic since Sam Daniels came into her life, only a couple of days ago, that she felt as if she were out of touch with the testing and lab work she was committed to.

She used her key to let herself into the main door, and after she entered she shut it behind her and locked it securely. It was still dark outside, and she knew the risks of someone, especially a woman, being by herself at this hour in Seattle. Better safe than sorry.

The normal lights were all out in the main corridors, and they were illuminated only by the nighttime running lights. The place always was a tad bit creepy after hours, and she always found herself walking at a very rapid pace to get to her office or lab during this time of day. Her nerves usually got the best of her when she was alone.

She let herself into her office and dropped off her briefcase and switched out her windbreaker for her lab coat. She started the coffee pot, which she always prepared in advance the night before, and as it started brewing she sat at the computer to check her email. Only a few important memos that were par for her department were what she found, so she made sure to read them thoroughly before deleting them.

Once her coffee was finished, she poured herself a stout cupful of the black liquid, grabbed her keys, and made her way down the corridor to the lab. The nighttime lights illuminated the room well, and she could see that the lab was in good order and clean. This was why she loved having Jason as an assistant: he left no stone unturned and took no shortcuts.

Once inside she flipped on the main lights and walked over to the desk she used in the lab; Jason's office was at the rear of the lab, and its door was closed, but to Kate's surprise the light inside was on. She knit her brow with concern. Was he already here? It certainly wasn't like him to leave any unnecessary lights on. She walked over to the door and rapped on it a couple of times before turning the knob. To her surprise, the door was unlocked.

Kate opened the door and took one step inside when she realized that Jason's office had been completely ransacked. All the doors on his filing cabinet were open, and the files inside had been scattered all over the floor. His desk was a complete disaster, with folders open and papers scattered everywhere. His desktop computer was on, but it was black. In a panic Kate ran to it and moved the mouse around; it lit up to show his lock screen, but there was no way to know if someone had accessed the unit or not.

Without a second thought, she picked up the receiver to the phone on his desk and dialed '9' before punching his cell number in furiously. Her breathing was erratic, and her heart continued to pound as she listened to his phone ringing in her ear.

"Hello?" It was Jason's voice, and he had obviously still been asleep.

"Jason!" Kate began, her voice was angry and high-pitched. "Did you leave your office completely demolished? It's a mess!"

His voice was still groggy when he answered, and she could tell he was trying to figure out who he was talking to. "Who's this? What office?"

Kate took a deep breath, then another. "Jason, it's Kate. I came in early today; remember I told you I was going to?"

"Oh, hi, Kate. Good morning."

Kate closed her eyes to control her temper. "No, Jason, it's not. When I came into the lab the light was on in your office, the door was unlocked, and all of your files have been ransacked!"

He didn't answer right away, and Kate knew he was trying to clear his head and understand what she was saying. Finally, he spoke, his voice a bit more aware. "My office?"

"Yes," Kate said. "Yes, Jason. Your office."

It was as though he were wide awake then. "What the…? I'll be there in a half-hour." The phone went dead in her hands, and Kate stared at the receiver helplessly before returning it to its cradle.

She looked around the room one last time. It would do her no good to snoop around; she had no idea what he had, or what would be missing if anything. She decided that she would check and feed the animals and record the required stats until he arrived.

It was hard for her to keep her mind on those tasks. She kept looking at the clock on the wall, and three times she spilled food on the floor as she went about doing her job. The task would have typically been completed in thirty minutes flat, but when Jason came running down the corridor to the lab just over a half-hour later, she was not even half-finished.

"What the heck is going on, Kate?" Jason's eyes were wide, and he was obviously angry.

Kate put down the clipboard, relieved that he was here. As they crossed the lab to get to his office all she said was, "You'll see."

He entered the office first and made it in only a step before he stopped, eyes afire and mouth wide open. "What the heck?"

"I told you, Jason." She stood in the doorway and watched him as he knelt down and shuffled through the mess of paper on the floor. "Who the heck would do something like this?"

Kate had already turned that over in her mind. There was nothing concerning their studies that would provoke this kind of offense. Their study was above-board in all aspects. It was definitely something else.

"Unless you are on drugs and owe your dealer, chances are it has to do with Sam Daniels and the bird," she said matter-of-factly. "What did you have here regarding that?"

Jason stood up and turned to her, his face red with fury. "I had a simple manila folder. It had one copy of the photo that he gave me, and it had about three sheets of handwritten notes in it that I had taken during our meetings on the matter."

Kate closed her eyes and shook her head. "Where was it? In the file cabinet?"

Jason immediately walked over to his desk and began to sort through the mess of papers which covered it. "No. It was on my desk."

He began to throw papers and folders here and there, glancing at each and every one, but they both knew, even before he was finished, that the file was going to be gone. Jason plopped down heavily in his desk chair and put his head in his hands. He looked as if he wanted to cry.

Kate pulled the chair across from him closer to the desk and sat down. She reached out and patted him on the arm. "Listen, we should have known. We should have expected Kreiger to go to these extremes."

"Good gosh," Jason replied, his voice cracking. "I sure didn't!"

Kate continued to pat his arm as he worked through his emotions. She wasn't angry at him. All this new information meant one thing and one thing only: Kate, Sam, and Jason were going to have to act fast, like immediately.

"Jason, I'm going to call Sam Daniels," she began. We were meeting him today to discuss travel plans anyway; we are just going to have to leave right away, rather than this weekend." She looked around the office in disgust, then continued. "I was planning on you going with us, but now you will have to stay here. There will be no time to find a trustworthy student to take care of the animals and the study; you are going to have to do it yourself. Rest assured you won't be left out of any credit given, understand?"

Jason looked up at her and nodded, his eyes moist with tears.

"I'm not mad, Jason. How the heck could you know?" She felt sorry for the young man who was so organized and meticulous. This was a crappy blow indeed.

"I'm going to my office to call Sam," Kate continued. "You stay here and get this room together. I'll be right back to wrap up the morning feeding and stats, okay?"

Jason nodded and stood from his desk. He bent down and picked up a single empty file folder, which he looked at with frustration before setting it on his desk and bending over for more. Kate stood and jogged out of the lab to her office. In minutes she had dialed Sam and was waiting for him to answer.

"Sam." His voice was very groggy, and Kate knew she had woken him up.

"Sam, it's Kate," she began. "Listen, I'm really sorry

to have disturbed your sleep so early, but we have a situation."

"Kate?" She could hear him shuffling around. "What's wrong? What's going on?"

Kate closed her eyes. How could Kreiger do something like this? The unscrupulous so-and-so was going to pay.

"Yes, Sam, we have a problem. I don't want to discuss it on the phone. Jason and I need you to come to the university as soon as possible."

Sam coughed on the other end. "Okay, okay. I'm up. I'm moving around. I'll just get a quick shower and…"

"No!" Kate replied, sitting forward in her desk, as if for emphasis. "I mean, now, Sam. That has to wait. You need to get here ASAP."

He was quiet for only a moment before he replied, "Okay, okay, Give me a half-hour, forty-five minutes or so, okay?"

Relieved, Kate agreed. She instructed him to call her cell phone when he arrived so she could let him in the building, then she hung up the phone. She would go to the lab and finish up the work there. Hopefully, Sam made good time.

They would have to leave as soon as possible, or Kreiger was going to steal everything right out from under their noses.

∞

Harold Kreiger sat on the sofa in the library at his private home. He was sipping coffee and enjoying the peace and quiet before heading to his office for the day.

A smile played on his face, and he hummed softly to himself. It was going to be a good day.

He reached his left hand out and began to caress an item on the sofa beside him: a manila file folder with the words 'Sam Daniels' written on the tab in black marker pen. His hand stroked it gently as if it were a lover. It might as well have been in Kreiger's mind.

It had been so much easier than he thought it would be. There was a student in one of his lecture classes, Kurt Strawn. Kurt came from a poor background, but he loved paleontology; he loved all things dinosaur. He had gotten into the university on scholarship, which was good for him because his parents couldn't have paid.

The thing about Kurt that Kreiger was aware of was his past. As a teen, Kurt had mingled with the wrong crowd for a short while and managed to get a couple of 'breaking and entering' charges on his record. They had been expunged, but Kreiger had taken the young man under his wing, and the details had been spilled openly as Kurt got to know the man.

It had been so easy. He would give Kurt one thousand dollars and a key to the zoology department, a universal key. Kurt had the nerve, and Kreiger supplied the means. Within an hour of putting the key in the boy's hand, Kreiger had his file.

It had almost been too easy.

Kreiger stood and went to the kitchen, where he warmed up his coffee before returning to the library. He had wanted to take a trip for some time, and now it looked like he was going to get his wish. Not only that, it was going to pay for him in more ways than one.

Looked like Harold Kreiger was going to the Amazonian jungle.

∞

Kate finished her lab work in a shorter time than she expected, and she decided to help Jason finish tidying up his office. The two of them were sorting papers and putting them in the appropriate folders when her cell vibrated loudly in her lab coat pocket.

"That'll be Sam, Jason," she said as she stood up to leave. "I'll go let him in. Be in my office in fifteen minutes, okay?"

Jason nodded, a strong look of defeat on his face. She walked over to him and patted his back gently. "No problem, Jason. It's okay. You have to let it go."

Kate left the room and walked quickly to the front of the building, where she found Sam practically hopping outside the main door. Fishing her keys out of her pocket she quickly let him in. Inside she turned to lock up.

"What the heck is going on, Kate?" Sam sounded confused and frustrated, but who wouldn't be?

She turned to him and took him by the arm to steer him toward her office. "Something has happened, but I don't want to talk about it until we are safe and sound in my office." She steered him all the way to her door, which she had to unlock. "Jason will be joining us in a bit."

Sam sat down. "You have coffee! Please, may I have some?"

"Absolutely," Kate replied. "Cream?"

Sam nodded. "So what's up, Kate? What's happened?"

She turned to him and handed him a full cup before having a seat at her desk. "Kreiger has been up to no good, Sam, and I'm afraid he may have gotten just what he wanted."

Sam sipped the coffee hungrily. "What do you mean?"

Kate sighed. "I came in early today to do some lab work. Jason's office had been broken into, and a file with the photo of the bird and handwritten notes he had taken had been stolen from off his desk."

Sam looked at Kate with his mouth open. "The guy broke in and stole things?"

Kate gave the nod and a slight shrug. "I mean, I can't prove it was him, but I am willing to bet my life savings on it, and I'm not a betting woman."

A sharp and rapid knock came on Kate's office door. "That'll be Jason," she said. "Come!"

Jason walked in, a forlorn look on his face. He grabbed a folding chair from the corner and opened it up next to Sam, then sat down. Sam could read his face, and he felt sorry for him. He could tell that the guy was completely blaming himself for what happened.

"Okay, guys," Kate began. "We now know what we are unfortunately dealing with when it comes to that rear end, Kreiger. There is no reason for us to cry over spilled milk, but we do need to make a plan that will allow us to act fast. I think I have it figured out."

"Go ahead then," Sam said, and he drained his coffee cup and stood to get more.

Kate nodded. "All right then. Kreiger now knows where you were when you encountered the animal. I can guarantee that his wheels are already turning. There is one thing I believe will be in our favor."

"What could that be?" Jason asked in a disgusted tone.

Sam sat back down, and Kate continued. "Kreiger is older, and he's been with the university for years and years, literally. I can promise you he will not pay for a flight out of his own pocket, but he will put in a requisition for the funds, probably immediately."

She stood and began to pace. "What this means is that it won't work for us to go on the university's tab, and that is just what he wants. We are going to have to pay for the trip ourselves, and we are going to have to do it right away, like yesterday." She stopped and looked at Sam. "Do you have the funds for such a trip?"

Sam nodded right away. "Oh, yeah. I have a pretty good savings stash, not to mention that I can likely get reimbursed by *Planet Geo* if we accomplish our goal."

Kate sat back at her desk. "I don't have a crap load of money, but I can pull it off. I already called last evening and got fair prices, just so I could put in a requisition myself, so I'm aware of the cost." Kate looked at Sam again. "Jason is going to stay; he'll have to take care of lab work. You and I will have to leave today if it is at all possible."

Jason let out a frustrated sigh and sat back in his

chair. "I know you're disappointed, Jason, and I'm sorry, but we don't have time to waste looking for a lab replacement," Kate said.

"I could just kill him," Jason said in a gruff voice. "Damn, if you only knew."

"Well," Kate continued, "now is the time for you to maintain and demonstrate self-control." She turned her attention back to Sam. "Are you ready for this?"

"Yes!" Sam replied. "I'd rather die than let a thieving bastard get away with anything! What do you want me to do?"

Kate leaned forward. "I have to contact records and take some time off. Say one week, to begin with; I have it coming. You know the hotels and other services we need so you will have to book those. I'll book our flights and cover them both, that way we will be able to sit together during our flight. You can reimburse me, okay?"

"Fine," Sam replied eagerly.

Kate turned back to Jason. "You have to act like everything is normal. If Kreiger thinks we are leaving, he will book his own ticket, and he will jump the gun on us. Don't let on anything, Jason. Nothing."

"I understand," he replied, and he stood up. "I'm gonna go back to the lab and finish my office. Let me know your flight plans, and if there is anything I can do to help." He turned around and left the office, his head hanging low.

"I'll tell you, Sam," Kate said as the door closed behind him. "If I thought it wouldn't give away our plans I would confront Kreiger right to his face today."

"I'd go with you," Sam agreed.

"Well, let's get on the phone and get these plans bought and paid for, what do you say?" Kate asked.

Sam smiled and pulled his cell out of his satchel. "I'm ready when you are."

R.W.K. Clark

CHAPTER 11

Kreiger sat at his desk, with Roy Hastings seated across from him. The man had a giddy smile on his face. "I can't believe it was so easy to get what we wanted," Hastings said.

"I knew we would get it done," Kreiger said. He was busy filling out requisition paperwork for the university. His own greed wouldn't even let him pay for his flight and accommodations. The university was going to foot the bill if he had anything to say about it.

He signed the bottom of the paper and looked up at Hastings, a satisfied, smug look filling his face. "I have to take these to the accounting department for approval. It typically takes them three or four days to approve, as you know, but I'm going to put a bit more pressure on them to speed things up. I'm claiming it as emergency travel."

Hastings stood and looked at his watch. It was getting close to lunch, and his stomach was growling miserably. "Did you include me?"

"Of course," Kreiger replied. "I wouldn't leave you out. You know that." The truth was he wished he could, but the man knew too much about how he had come to possess location information. It wouldn't do to piss him off. He would sweep him under the rug soon enough.

Kreiger stood as well, paperwork in hand. The two men left the office and made their way out to the parking lot and their vehicles. "Let me know how it goes," Hastings said before they parted ways.

Kreiger gave the nod. "Sure thing." He then dug his car keys out of his pocket and made his way across the lot to his car.

He was about ten feet from it when a small, beat-up car pulled up beside him. He was busy fishing for the right key on the ring and didn't notice right away.

"Dr. Kreiger, how are you today?"

He looked up. It was Jason Seward, Kate Beck's assistant. Kreiger wanted to laugh out loud, but he controlled himself.

"Fine, Jason. How are you?"

"Awesome," he replied. "Looks like the sun is going to peek out today for a change."

Kreiger looked skyward, then back at Jason. "Did you come to see me?"

"Oh, no," he said. "I was leaving campus for lunch."

Kreiger thought he saw a funny look on Jason's face, as though he were mocking him in his mind. Surely he had been in his office already. Why was he not saying anything about the break-in?

"Where's Kate?" Kreiger asked, key in hand.

Jason smiled at him and held his eyes. "Oh, she's way busy. A couple of the new animals are sick, and she's tending to them. The way it looks, she won't even be able to focus on Sam Daniels and his stuff. Probably not until next week, at the soonest."

"Oh," Kreiger said, his heart growing excited. "I'm sorry to hear that. I hope it all clears up for her."

"Me too," Jason said. "You have a good day now, Dr. Kreiger."

Kreiger nodded. "You too, Jason." With that he turned away, dismissing Jason and the conversation.

Jason drove away from Kreiger, a self-satisfied grin plastered to his face. Now the paleontologist wouldn't feel a need to rush for the tickets. Jason noticed the paper in his hand, and it had definitely been a requisition application. After all, Jason had filled out enough of them.

He had planted the seed. Now he felt certain that Kate and Sam would have a decent head start, and that was all he wanted. To screw over Kreiger for what he had done felt like so much poetic justice.

∞

Kate and Sam had just finished reserving their tickets and making all the needed reservations.

Sam looked up at her. She was writing all the details down in a spiral notebook. "So," he began. "Are you… hungry at all?"

Kate looked up and closed the notebook before locking in the desk drawer. She smiled at him. "I am, as a matter of fact. I'm famished."

"Would you want to have lunch with me? I mean, we're leaving first thing in the morning. We can actually relax a bit, you know?" He was nervous asking her out;

he didn't have a lot of practice with the opposite sex.

"Sure," she replied. "Where do you want to go?"

"How about a fast food joint?" he asked. He knew it wasn't romantic, but he had seen several fast food bags in her garbage, and he assumed she liked it. "I was thinking something quick."

Kate stood, her eyes lighting up. "I love that idea. I guess you could say I'm not the healthiest person on the planet, but I'm satisfied."

The two headed out, their stress alleviated for the time being. Soon they would be on their way. Soon they would be stepping into their future.

∞

Kreiger stood at the counter of the budgeting office stapling a copy of the photo of the bird and Jason Seward's notes, which he had rewritten in his own hand, to the requisition. Jane Ross, the head of accounting at the university, waited patiently for him to hand the paperwork over. He looked her in the eye when he did.

"Because of the situation with the death of an individual, it is essential that we try to get this approved as soon as possible," Kreiger said.

"Well, it sounds exciting, Harold, but also dangerous," Jane replied.

Kreiger nodded. "Yes, but I told them I would be there by next weekend at the latest. They are a bit desperate."

"Well," Jane replied, "you know that approval normally takes five to seven days. I'll try to rush it, but the worst-case scenario will place you in Brazil by next

Wednesday."

"That will be fine," Kreiger said. "Thanks for your help."

She smiled at him. She had a bit of a crush on Kreiger years ago, and even now she got a little flighty around him, even though she had married two years ago. "If I don't see you before you leave, have a safe trip, and come back in one piece."

"Of course," Kreiger said. He left the office feeling like a huge weight was lifted from his shoulders. This was going to go off without a hitch; he just knew it.

When he got back to his office, he called Hastings. He told him the requisition was in, and he repeated what Jane Ross had told him regarding approval. It was going to be smooth sailing.

"Do you know if Collins has time in her schedule to take over a couple of my lectures?" He asked Hastings this because Hastings had a thing for Marie Collins. If anyone knew he would.

"Hmmm," Hastings replied thoughtfully. "You'll have to ask her. You have her extension, I'm sure."

"Yes, I'll just give her a ring," he said. "Talk to you soon."

He struggled to keep from laughing out loud. Thankfully not everyone was as slick as he was. He loved it.

He was going to die a very, very rich man.

"So," Sam was saying, "have you ever been married? Have any kids?" He poked a couple of French fries into his mouth and waited for Kate to answer.

She finished chewing a bite of a massive chicken, cheddar, and bacon sandwich. "No on both. My career has been my focal point for as long as I can remember."

"Mine too," he replied. "I can honestly say I never really even gave it any thought." Until I met you, Sam thought to himself.

Kate's cell began to ring in her jacket pocket. She retrieved it and answered the call. "Jason! I should have asked you if you wanted me to bring you anything."

"That's okay, Kate," Jason said. "I already ate. Listen, I called to tell you that I ran into Kreiger as he was leaving his office earlier."

Kate looked at Sam and gave him a conspiratorial grin. "Really? What did that larcenous bastard have to say?"

"He was carrying a requisition form, among other papers. He's putting in for funds, Kate."

"I see," she replied, her smile fading.

"I told him a bunch of your animals got sick when he asked after you," Jason continued. "I also led him to believe you wouldn't even be able to leave with Daniels for at least a week, maybe more. I hope you booked a flight. You can beat him down there."

"What a coincidence!" Kate said. "We leave first thing in the morning."

Jason laughed out loud. "Good," he replied finally.

"Serves him right. I'm gonna go. See you when you get here."

Kate disconnected and relayed what Jason had said to Sam. They had a good laugh over it as they finished their lunch. Their spirits were much lighter now, at least compared to that morning.

As they ate and talked, Sam had thoughts all his own; thoughts about the beautiful black-haired lady in front of him. What did she like to do in her spare time? What kind of men did she like? Did she like to travel?

Kate, too, had her own mental agenda. Sam had the softest-looking hair she had ever seen, and his eyes could melt diamonds. He was smart, and a good conversationalist. She wondered if he had a girlfriend.

They left together, talking about their trip and the bird they would be chasing. They were comfortable with each other, and Kate knew that even professionally it was a great match. They could conquer the world together.

If everything went their way, anyway.

R.W.K. Clark

CHAPTER 12

Sam was at home packing, and for the first time, he was struggling with what he should take.

He never gave thought to his attire when he worked, but he had never been in the company of a beautiful, intelligent scientist. He didn't want to appear grubby or careless, but he also didn't want to look like he was trying to impress her. Kate Beck had Sam Daniels tied up in knots. It seemed that the true purpose of their trip, and Sam's passion for it, had faded into the shadows cast by the light of Dr. Kate Beck.

After an hour of struggling, he looked at the clock. Damn, he had been at it for way too long! It was six in the evening, and he had to be at the airport with Kate at four thirty in the morning. He began to toss his usual attire in the suitcase; it would have to do.

Sam put his bags by the door and made sure he had his passport and other necessary documents before tossing a fried chicken TV dinner in the microwave. He had promised himself that he would start eating better, but it seemed that life had dealt him a few too many curve balls for him to focus properly on correcting his poor diet. Kate certainly didn't look like she lived off frozen foods; he would hate to embarrass himself by inviting her over for a mini-feast served in a black plastic tray.

He shook his head as he pulled the dinner out midway and stirred the potatoes. This woman was consuming his thoughts; he hadn't even been thinking about Rico or the bird, at least, not half as much as one would expect. The fact brought a smile to his face, but he knew he was going to have to focus if he was going to be at all effective while back in the jungle, and Kate would need him to be effective. So would the rest of the world, as a matter of fact.

Sam turned the news on and opened up a TV tray to eat on. He wanted to watch the weather and see how things were looking in the Amazon. He would have already done this a couple of weeks ago; it was definitely time to snap out of it.

∞

Kate relaxed in a hot bubble bath in the bathroom at her apartment. She was satisfied with her packing, having done a ton of research into the area. It hadn't been too hard to plan what to take at all once she had a firm grasp on what to expect in the jungle.

They would stay in a hotel the first night; after that, when she and Sam headed into the jungle itself, they would have a guide with them. Sam let her know that the owner of the guide company, a place called Expedition Amazon, would also be accompanying the pair as well, and he and the guide would be armed. Kate felt much better knowing that, and it helped her to relax.

She lifted her large, soft sponge from the water and squeezed it over her chest. This was just what she needed to calm down and rest her mind. For most of the day she had fretted herself over Kreiger and Hastings, seething with anger over the lengths they were going to in their effort to steal Sam's discovery. It was infuriating to her, as it reflected badly on everyone involved. It was a relief that Sam had come to her first.

Now her mind drifted to him, the photographer who had entered her life so suddenly and unexpectedly. He was a looker, that was for sure, and as she got to know him, bit by bit, a little better, she found herself impressed with his personal focus: like her, his career was paramount. She admired this and found it more than a little attractive. Maybe after this was over the two of them could spend some time together on a more social basis.

Her water was cooling faster than she would have liked. She sat up and pulled the plug and set it on the side of the tub before climbing out and wrapping her towel around herself. She caught a bit of a chill, and her skin broke out in goosebumps, so she toweled off quickly and put a big fluffy white robe on before padding to the living room to watch a bit of television.

She had just tuned in CNN when her cell phone chirped. She retrieved it from the counter in the kitchen and looked at the screen; it was Sam Daniels. Kate smiled as she slid her finger across the screen of the smartphone to answer the call.

"Hello?"

Sam cleared his throat nervously. "Um, hi, Kate. It's Sam."

"Hi, Sam," she replied. "What's up?"

His voice gave away the trepidation he felt in calling her; he simply didn't have enough experience with women to boldly speak to her with confidence. "I was, um, just wondering how your packing is coming along?"

"Fine," Kate said. "I've been done for a while. I actually invested some time in familiarizing myself with the region we are visiting. I can only hope the things I've packed will be sufficient."

Sam shook his head at himself in disgust. "I'm so sorry," he said. "I should have thought to let you know about the area. I've been far too spaced-out for my own good, or anyone else's, for that matter."

"No worries, Sam," Kate replied. "I'm pretty sure I'll be fine."

"Have you had dinner?" he asked.

Kate padded back to the living room with the phone. "Yes, as a matter of fact, I ate fairly early. I'm going to watch a bit of news and hit the sack early. How about you?"

"Yeah," Sam said. "I already ate too. Checking the weather forecast for where we are going, then I'm turning in myself." He went quiet for a moment, and Kate patiently waited. "Guess I just wanted to see how you were doing and tell you I'd see you in the morning. Picking you up at three thirty, right? Bitter Lake, apartment 322, right?"

Kate smiled at the eagerness in his voice because it matched her own. "Right, Sam. See you at three-thirty."

"Bye, Kate." Sam disconnected, and Kate found herself looking at the phone in her hand with amusement.

She returned her phone to the charger on the kitchen counter and checked her coffee pot to make sure the automatic timer was set. Suddenly she gave a big yawn; there had been so much excitement in her life that she would likely sleep very well that night, she knew. She wanted to, because who knew what the next few days would hold for her?

It took Kate only a minute to decide against watching television. She turned off the box and double-checked the lock on her apartment door before heading into her bedroom and climbing naked between her sheets. She found comfort in only a few moments, and soon she drifted off to sleep, her excitement fueling her dreams.

∞

Harold Kreiger was asleep, but he tossed restlessly on his bed. His dreams were distant and anxiety-ridden. He seemed to be chasing something that remained just out of his reach, like a rabbit pursuing a carrot on a string, and it was enough to drive him mad.

Suddenly the telephone on his nightstand rang loudly. He jerked out of his semi-slumber right away, but the phone rang two more times before Harold realized what was going on and reached for the receiver. His alarm clock read two-thirty in the morning in bright red digits; who was calling him at this time of night?

"Hello!" Kreiger snarled into the telephone. He wanted to let whoever it was known just what he thought of their untimely intrusion.

"Harold, it's Roy, Roy Hastings."

Kreiger swung his legs over the side of the bed. "Hold on, Roy." He covered the mouthpiece and began coughing almost uncontrollably. Roy winced on the other end as he listened. Obviously, Kreiger was still smoking.

Kreiger gave one last cough then put the receiver back to his ear. "What's going on?"

"Well," Hastings began, "I was having a hard time sleeping, and I got up to watch the news and surf the Internet a bit. Harold, I got a call from my nephew Rob. You know, the one that I had watching the airline bookings."

Now Kreiger took a couple of gulps of water from a glass next to his bed. "Yeah? And?"

"It looks like our little Dr. Beck and her friend Daniels are leaving on a four-thirty flight to the Amazonian jungle, my friend."

Now Kreiger was wide-awake, and he felt his skin begin to prickle with panic. "What? They're flying out tonight? In only a couple of hours? We need to be on that damn plane, Roy!" He stood and began to pace back and forth in the dark room.

"I already thought of that, Harold, and I called to book a couple of flights, but they aren't booking anymore for that particular plane," Roy said. "We have to leave on the next one, and that isn't until the same time tomorrow morning."

"What the heck!" Kreiger was furious, just as Hastings knew he would be. He grabbed the telephone's base and turned on the lamp before he resumed pacing. "Let me think, just let me think. Did you book a couple of seats?"

"No, and we will have to have inoculations and take care of all kinds of other stuff before we can go," Hastings said with a weary sigh. "I wanted to talk to you first. Those two have been on top of their game, and now we need to get in gear."

Kreiger forced himself to calm down. "Okay, okay," he began. "You get arrangements made for all of that; I'll keep my calendar clear. But make sure you let me know every last detail that needs attention because the university is sure gonna foot the bill, my friend. I'm up now, so tell me what I have to do."

Kreiger fished a tablet and pen out of the drawer in his nightstand and began writing an itemized list, as Hastings spouted into the phone. When he was finished, he made plans with Roy regarding appointments that needed to be made, including Kreiger paying a visit to the budgeting department to speed up the approval process.

Finally, they disconnected the call, and Harold went directly into the bathroom to shower. He certainly wouldn't be able to sleep anymore tonight; there was no time. Those two slippery snakes had managed to get the jump on him, and he wasn't about to let them get any more of a head start than they already had.

No, he was already figuring out how to close the gap as quickly as possible.

CHAPTER 13

Kate and Sam sat, buckled securely in their seats, listening to the pilot welcome them on the flight. Both were extremely relieved that they were taking off, especially without Kreiger or one of his minions in accompaniment. Looks like they had done things the right way.

They would fly from Seattle to Chicago, then go from O'Hare in Chicago to Miami. Next they would hit Rio de Janeiro, and finally, they would fly for five or six hours to Manaus. There they would check into a hotel for a single night, and in the morning Manuel Pereira from Expedition Amazon would pick them up, and they would meet up with one of his guides.

They would be meeting at the entrance that Rico had taken him to, to the same road the man had died on.

It was at this point in the plan that Sam began to get very nervous indeed, and for obvious reasons. He refused to let Kate see his stress, however. He wanted her calm and sensible, just as he was determined to be. It would do neither of them any good, or anyone else, for that matter, if Sam were a nervous wreck, and it would breed nervousness in all those around him.

As if on cue Kate touched his arm. "How are you feeling, Sam?"

He reached up and gave her hand a pat and flashed her a smile. "I'm as good as could be expected, but I feel much better than I thought I would."

Kate held his eyes as if studying him and weighing his words. Finally, she raised her eyebrows, grinned, and said, "Liar."

Sam threw his head back and gave her a hearty laugh. After a moment he pulled himself together. "Really, Kate, I'm good. It will be a relief to take care of this. You know, identify it and study it. To find out what we are facing, and I don't mean just you and I." He patted her hand once more for good measure and took a deep breath. "I can't tell you how relieved I am that you are with me."

Kate didn't know what to say. Part of her was flattered; he was basically grateful for the education she had and the willingness she was exhibiting to join him on this mission. But Kate knew that, no matter how much interest and devotion and concern she had shown, there was another part of her whose motives were basically selfish. Upon hearing his heartfelt thanks, she felt a level of embarrassment and shame that she was not accustomed to feeling.

She smiled and rubbed his arm a bit before pulling her hand away. "Sam, I want to do this. I want to help in any way I can, and hopefully, I can be of some benefit. But you do know that my interests are somewhat… personal, as well, don't you?"

Sam's smile stayed on his face, but his hand fell away from hers, his head leaned back against his headrest, and he gazed at the bottom of the overhead compartments as if they were filled with the wonders of the known universe. "Yeah," he responded, his voice a bit distant. "I'm not a stupid man. I suppose I have known that all along, but I certainly trust the interest and care you have demonstrated far more than that of your esteemed colleagues."

Kate picked up on the slight bit of sarcasm in his voice, and for reasons, she couldn't understand her heart sank. She looked down at her hands in her own lap, ashamed to look up. She had basically just admitted her own lack of integrity, no matter how small, and she wondered if she had damaged the small existing level of trust that was between them.

Sam elbowed her lightly in the arm, and she looked up at him, trying to hold back the small tears that were threatening to escape from behind her eyelids. "I just didn't want us to be working side by side, doing this… the thing we are doing, without you understanding me wholly and completely," she said.

"I'm pretty sure I had already thought of all that," he replied. "Now that the air is clear, we can go forward and deal with this just the way we had intended. Right, Kate?" He elbowed her again for good measure.

"Right, Sam." She elbowed him back, and the two of them broke into giggles under their breath like a couple of high school students just getting to know each other.

It was right at that moment that Sam knew whatever hopes he had for getting to know Dr. Kate Beck were all well and good. At that exact same moment, Kate knew the same thing. They both felt relief, and they were able to settle into their own personal mode of comfort from that second on, for the rest of the flight.

They arrived at O'Hare soon enough, and they both had to hustle to get to the right concourse to board their connecting flight on time. They got there just in time, with a line of passengers already showing their tickets, antsy to board and get settled in. Both Sam and Kate barely had time to catch their breath before it was their turn to hand over their tickets for approval. They stowed their carry-ons and plopped into their seats with hardly moments to spare, and they found themselves laughing breathlessly at how winded they both were.

The flight to Miami was a bit more entertaining. Now Kate had enough with the uncomfortable silence between them, and she was determined to put Sam back at ease with her. Perhaps she had divulged a bit too much during the first leg of their flight, but she was going to make it right. She found that her interest, in this case, had more to it than just her own chances for fame and fortune. No, she was quite aware of the feelings she was developing for Mr. Sam Daniels, and for some reason, she found herself unwilling to let them simply evaporate like so much steam or mist. She wanted to pursue the emotions she was experiencing.

So, she stepped up to the plate and began to break the ice. She joked and teased. She intentionally kept the purpose for their trip out of the conversation, even when Sam, in his discomfort, interjected with such. She went out of her way to touch him or poke at him, and it did not escape her attention when he obviously enjoyed it. Kate's extroverted personality became the strong point, especially when the reality set in that neither of them really knew what they were doing when it came to the opposite sex. She was more than willing to follow her instincts and let them guide her, even if he was overwhelmed with shyness.

Once they were in Miami, they had a bit more time to get to their connecting flight, as the layover was a bit more extensive. "How about we get a drink?" Kate asked him as they made their way through the crowds in the general direction they were heading.

Sam actually smiled a bit at the suggestion. Neither of them had indulged in any alcohol on either leg of their flight yet; obviously, they weren't die-hard drinkers. "I think that is an incredible idea," he replied. The truth was that he could use a little help. He wasn't stupid; Kate was flirting, and while he was enjoying it immensely he seemed to be stuck, and he was keenly aware of it. A little sauce would help him relax and go with the flow.

They found a restaurant with a bar, and both agreed it would be an ideal spot. "I love Mexican food," Sam shared as they were seated. "I would much rather grab a bite here than try to struggle my way through a plane tray. How about you?"

"The truth is I haven't flown in a while," Kate

admitted. "I probably wouldn't have known the difference."

Sam laughed out loud. "You don't need experience flying to know that the food is sadly lacking."

They got comfortable at a smaller table for two, and both of them ordered margaritas with crushed ice. "It has been so long since I had one of these," Kate said. "I have to admit, I'm a bit excited. Maybe I'm having too much fun already."

Color came to Sam's cheeks at her words. "Me too," he said shyly, avoiding her eyes a bit. Their waitress set their drinks down in front of them, and taking notice of their closed menus asked, "Are you two ready to order?"

Kate came to her senses then and giggled a bit. "I'm sorry," she said to the girl. "I'm afraid we haven't even looked at them yet." She kept her eyes on Sam as she spoke, and the server took notice.

Smiling, the girl said, "I'll just give you two a bit more time."

"Thanks," Sam offered as he held Kate's eyes right back. The girl left, and he continued, "Maybe we should actually see what is on the menu."

For the next few minutes they scanned the available options, then finally, for the first time, Sam seemed to take the upper hand a bit. "How about if we have a plate of Kicking Nachos and share them?"

"I think that sounds amazing." Kate also loved Mexican food, and sharing a plate of nachos with the gorgeous man in front of her seemed almost like the perfect 'first date,' even if that wasn't what their meal was all about. She had a feeling that they were both looking at it as such.

They ordered, and the food came quickly. They ate and laughed, and both of them discovered that they loved each other's company immensely. Sam found Kate to be quick-witted and eager to put him at ease, on top of being beautiful and intelligent. Once he loosened up, Kate enjoyed his own sense of humor and ability to laugh at her goofy jokes. Forgetting about work was a much-needed freedom neither of them had the luxury of experiencing for quite some time, and it was heaven.

The time flew, and soon it would be time to head back. Thankfully both of them were done drinking after one margarita, and they actually had a good little buzz.

∞

They found their concourse area and arrived ahead of time, so they sat patiently, a short distance from everyone else, and engaged in getting to know each other a bit better.

"So, where did you go to college, Sam?" Kate was genuinely interested in him and longed to know what put him on the path he walked today. She turned sideways in her chair so she could face him and give him her full attention.

"Well," he began, "my grandmother gave me my first camera, and it seemed really natural to me, so that became my focus very early in life. She died when I was seventeen, but not before she basically made me love the art. I ended up studying photography at the

Academy of Art in San Francisco, and the rest is history."

"You were close to her," Kate observed. "Did she raise you?"

Sam shrugged. "Technically, no, but if you are genuinely asking I would have to say yes." He looked down at his hands and fiddled with his fingers. Kate could tell his grandmother was still a painful subject for him. "How about you?"

"Born in Seattle, raised in Seattle, studied zoology and ornithology at UW," she said simply. "Interned there, and have worked there ever since. I took over as head of my department, the youngest ever, I proudly add, when Dr. Adeline Hoover passed away eighteen months ago. She was my mentor, and I miss her, but she pretty much taught me everything I know."

"Why birds?" He asked, his eyes searching her face as he tried to read her and get to know her.

Kate smiled at him and leaned forward conspiratorially. "Because they are free," she whispered with a smile, then she leaned in even more and kissed him softly on the lips.

Sam's eyes closed automatically, and his body broke out in gooseflesh. Her lips were as soft as silk, and she smelled like baby powder: fresh and innocent. Oh, wow, I think I'm in love with this woman, he thought to himself.

Kate pulled away and smiled, blood rushing to her cheeks. Wow, she thought, this is the one.

"All passengers taking Flight 375 to Rio de Janeiro

who need special assistance or have small children will begin boarding in five minutes. Please be ready with tickets; we will call all other passengers shortly after. Thank you." The clipped and formal female voice pumping through the speakers was enough to snap them out of their reverie.

"I guess we had better get ourselves together," Kate said.

All Sam could do was a nod in agreement as he smiled like a goofball. He grabbed his carry-on, and she did the same, even though the line forming told them it would be a bit before they were called. Kate turned around in her chair and faced forward, and Sam sat up a bit himself. It was time to pay attention and straighten up, but neither of them wanted to. They continued to sneak looks at each other out of the corner of their eyes, and whenever they caught each other, they giggled like children.

After fifteen minutes the rest of those waiting were called for boarding, and soon Kate and Sam were taking their seats and buckling in. Kate was near the window, which she loved, but she had been next to the window the entire trip. "So, Sam, do you want to have the window seat for a change?"

"You know," he replied, "I fly quite often, and I know you don't, so I'm fine if you are."

She nodded, relieved. "Thanks." She took his hand and squeezed it, and continued to hold it. Sam didn't put up a fight. Her small hands were soft, warm, and dry, and he found it oddly comforting.

As the pilot went through his spiel, Sam closed his eyes and leaned his head back. He thought about the incident that had brought him to this day, sitting here next to Kate Beck, and for the first time since they had left Seattle, his heart felt a tug of grief for Rico and his family. Pictures of the bird and the violence it inflicted on his guide flashed through his mind, and he had to open his eyes wide and shake his head to get rid of them. The last thing he was going to do was relive that terror over and over again. After all, the trip was about taking control of a situation that had already proven deadly. He wouldn't shrink away in fear or grief.

Kate fell asleep very soon after the flight got underway, and Sam enjoyed watching her. It kept his mind off his own tormenting thoughts, and allowed him to have a hope for his future that he hadn't, as of yet, pondered hardly at all. Just looking at her peacefully sleeping, and remembering her soft kiss at the airport, was enough to do the trick, and he found himself mentally reliving it over and over again.

Sam felt very happy for the first time in a long time.

∞

By the time Sam and Kate were getting off the plane in Rio and preparing to catch their final flight to Manaus, Kreiger and Hastings were boarding their own flight at SeaTac airport. Harold Kreiger had tried to put pressure on the budgeting department to push his requisition through, but to no avail. He'd had to pay for his own ticket, and due to some credit problems Hastings seemed to be having, he'd ended up lending his associate the money for his ticket as well. He was pissed off and impatient.

They were a full day behind Kate and that Daniels fellow, but that was the least of Kreiger's worries. While he had the notes that Jason Seward had taken, and they were quite thorough, he had no idea where the pair would be staying or even the precise location where they would begin their search. The fact was he was going to have to do a bit of manipulating and smooth talking to find out the information he wanted and needed if he was going to succeed in his plan to usurp those two.

He reminded himself that he was one of the smartest men he knew, and he would succeed, regardless of resistance. This was simply the chance of a lifetime for him. The creature was no more a 'bird' than a monkey. Kreiger knew that what he had looked at had to be directly descended from the archaeopteryx if it wasn't one through and through. To Kreiger that meant that what was being dealt with was technically a dinosaur, and dinosaurs were his department. Kate needed to stay at home and study migrating geese or something. She was out of her element with this situation.

Hastings seemed almost sick when they were in the air. He was a bit green around the gills, and whenever they hit a pocket of turbulence the man would moan and groan. Kreiger figured it was best to let him struggle through it; after all, they had quite a flight plan ahead of them. He filled his time with note taking and journaling about the situation at hand. He recorded what he already knew and added to what he had already recorded. When he felt emotional turmoil over the resistance, Kate and Daniels were giving him he recorded that as well, and much of his 'journaling' consisted of angry rants and whining about how unfair the situation was.

So the two men went through the motions required to get from Seattle to Manaus, and they did it mostly in silence. The entire series of flights would span over a few days; he had bought bargain fares, and he could only hope the two ahead of them had done the same. This was just another point he found himself angrily fretting over. Had he been aware that Sam and Kate indeed had purchased the same type of flight plan he would have allowed himself to relax a bit.

But for now, he was consumed with how he would succeed in catching up…

CHAPTER 14

Sam and Kate arrived in Manaus on Sunday night, and after being on one airplane or another, or at least stiff, uncomfortable seats in airports since early Thursday morning, they were both more than ready to check into their hotel and get some sleep in a comfortable bed.

Sam had booked two rooms at the Continental Hotel. He had stayed there several times, and while it wasn't top of the line, it was clean and comfortable. Their rooms were side by side, so he felt fine about being able to keep a protective eye on Kate, and they were able to get a taxi to the accommodations easily enough. During the ride, Sam went over the plan for the next day.

"We'll get a good night's sleep," he began. "We'll be able to clean up, which you will want to take advantage of. Lord knows how long we are going to be out there."

Kate listened intently and jotted notes as he spoke. The last thing she wanted was to lose track of him while she was in the middle of Brazil. "You said the men from the guide company will pick us up, or will we rent a car and go to them?"

"Miguel Pereira will be picking us up at ten in the morning," he replied. "Oh, that reminds me: he and his men will be bringing food, but it will be bare bones; I pay them to do that. You will want to order a meal to go to take with you from the café. It will likely be the last one you have for a while."

Kate jotted this down as well, then said, with slight embarrassment, "Um, Sam, I don't speak Portuguese. I barely speak Spanish."

Sam gave her a grin and a pat on the shoulder. "Stick with me. I'll take care of you."

His words gave her a pleased chill. She closed her notebook and sat back, literally feeling safer than she had since leaving Seattle. He said he would take care of her, and she thoroughly believed him.

The hotel turned out to be better than Kate expected. For some reason, likely lack of experience, she had a visual in her head that told her the rooms would be very bare-bones and un-accommodating. They were small but clean and comfortable, contrary to her preconceived notion. She knew she could trust Sam, but she had been fiercely independent for so long that it seemed she thought herself the only capable person in her life.

Sam walked her to her room and unlocked the door for her, then carried in her bags. He did a quick walkthrough before stating, "Everything looks great here." He turned to her before leaving. "If you get a yen for anything don't hesitate to call my room. Since this is your first time, you shouldn't wander about alone, okay?"

Kate nodded and smiled. "No problem." She didn't feel any temptation to venture out on her own; she was just too far from home to try to go it alone.

"Well," Sam said, "I guess I'm going to head next door." He paused at her door, looking just a bit unsure. He wanted to kiss her, and Kate was thinking the same thing, but they were both as nervous as schoolkids.

She stood smiling with her arms crossed over her chest while Sam shifted his weight nervously from one foot to the other. Finally, Kate took the upper hand. She took a single step toward him and popped up onto her tiptoes. She tilted her face upward and looked him right in the eye before planting her lips firmly on his, and that was all it took.

In no time the door to her room was closed, and they were kissing with such heat and passion that you would have thought they were long-lost lovers who'd just found each other after years of fruitless searching. Sam felt slight trepidation, and because of it, he didn't let his hands do the wandering they wanted to, but Kate held nothing back. She allowed her own hands to roam up and down his back and over his rear, stopping there and squeezing with passion. She found she wanted to take all of the details of Sam Daniels in, soaking them up like so much warm sunlight.

Her tongue teased its way into his mouth, and Sam didn't offer any resistance. He tasted her, and she tasted fresh and clean. He felt her firm breasts pressing against his chest, her nipples poking at him through their shirts, and he was unable to control the erection that was growing in his trousers.

Kate wasn't trying to control anything. She wasn't a virgin; she had dated a young man in college for nearly two years, but he had been lazy and had no drive. Since breaking up with him she had abstained, and she had absolutely no desire to do so right now. She pressed herself harder against his hips, letting him know how she felt in no uncertain terms.

Sam simply melted, and he knew that Kate Beck was exactly what he wanted.

Finally, she pulled away from him and looked him in the eye, holding his gaze with a strength he didn't know she possessed. She took her jacket off and began to undo her white button-down shirt. When it was open, his eyes went to the curve of her breasts, and he found himself entranced with the way her lace bra held them and caressed them. She unbuttoned her jeans then, and Sam let out a groan that he could not contain.

Kate smiled as she kicked off her shoes and took off her jeans a leg at a time. Sam was frozen in place, or so it seemed to him. He watched her take off her shirt, and then Kate stood before him in her white bra and panties. He could hardly breathe.

She was perfect. Her belly was flat and muscled, and her skin was a gorgeous shade of tan that set off her hair and eyes. She turned her back to him and pulled back the blanket and sheet on her bed, then she sat on its edge and removed her underclothing. Sam still hadn't moved a muscle.

Kate smiled at him, then walked to him, completely naked and stunning. She wrapped her arms around his neck and began to kiss him so passionately he broke out in a sweat. Her little body squirmed hotly against his own, and as she kissed him, she turned him around and began to back him toward the bed.

At that point, Sam decided he would let her steer, and he succumbed to her leadership. He felt the back of his thighs come in contact with the bed, and his legs buckled. He fell backward, Kate still clinging to him and exploring his mouth with her own. He began to have serious doubts that he would be able to contain himself much longer; it was becoming almost painful.

As if she read his mind Kate pulled herself off of him and stood next to the bed looking down at him. Her smile was strong on her face, and her eyes were smoky with passion. She reached down and tugged at the button on his trousers; it gave with no resistance. Before it even registered in his mind his pants were gone.

Surprisingly to Sam he felt absolutely no embarrassment. Quite the contrary; he couldn't wait to be completely rid of the clothes that suddenly felt so damn confining he thought he would strangle. Kate positioned herself between his knees and grasped his shirt by the collar. She gave one solitary pull backward, and the buttons went flying. That move alone nearly threatened to end it all for him; she was the sexiest thing he had ever laid eyes on.

Now Sam lay on the bed, his shirt torn open and his

pants around his ankles. He was so stupefied by her that he had forgotten that he still sported his boxer briefs, but the fact had not evaded Kate. She straddled his waist and pressed herself against him, kissing him purposefully, all the while inching his briefs down his hips. Soon they were in the middle of his thighs, and she wasted no more time. She positioned herself over him, and with a bit of guidance and a single move he was up inside of her, buried deep.

Oh, yes, Sam thought, almost on the verge of panic. I'm going to lose it I swear. Kate seemed to be reading his mind, and she stopped moving, but only until his breathing steadied. Little did he know she was on the verge herself, but she didn't care about personal appearances. She waited only a short moment, then her hips moved up and down on him with such dedication that neither of them could hold back any longer.

They exploded together almost violently, their thrusting reaching almost violent levels. Sam's groans were loud, and just listening to him brought her off easily once again. They continued to move together, moaning, sweat trickling over their skin until there was nothing left to move to, and then Kate collapsed on top of him, her eyes closed and a smile glued to her face.

It had been a long time, for both of them.

The next five minutes passed in silence, then Kate pushed herself up. She looked down at him and grinned. "Sorry if I took advantage of you, but, oh wait. No, I'm not."

They both laughed loudly, and Kate was still

laughing when she stood and went into the bathroom and closed the door. Sam couldn't even move, though he kept telling himself to get up. If he wasn't in love before the deal was certainly sealed now.

He groaned and sat up. His shirt was missing three buttons, and his underwear was tightly wrapped around his thighs. He stood and nearly fell down because of his trousers, which had completely engulfed his feet and ankles. He got his wits about him and managed to pull it all together. Sam ended up removing his shirt and tossing it into a wastebasket next to the small writing desk, after which he began to rummage through his suitcase for a new one.

He was pulling a clean t-shirt over his head when the bathroom door opened. Kate was standing in the light with a bath towel around her. "You know, Sam, I find it senseless that you booked two rooms. Also, do you know how much water we could save by showering together?"

Sam turned around and looked at her before pulling his t-shirt back off. He smiled as he approached her and planted his mouth on hers. The two of them backed into the bathroom and closed the door.

"Welcome to Brazil, Dr. Beck," he whispered against her mouth as the bathroom door latched shut.

R.W.K. Clark

CHAPTER 15

The next morning at eight Kate and Sam went down to the front desk, where Sam used his credit card to book Kate's room for the next seven days. As she slept he had done some thinking; his possessions were appropriate for the trip, but her bags were a bit too bulky for their excursion. When she woke they narrowed down what they would take on the tour, packed it together, and decided to keep the room so their things would be safe and sound.

Next, they put in two orders to go for simple sandwich plates from room service, which were brought to them all bagged up. The staff was knowledgeable of Sam and his needs, and Kate saw that they were very expeditious in serving him. In no time they had everything they needed, and they were seated in the lobby waiting to be picked up by Miguel Pereira.

He arrived ten minutes before ten, and though he sported a very serious look on his face, he was quite kind and accommodating. He and Sam exchanged a manly embrace before Sam introduced him and Kate.

"Miguel, this is Dr. Beck," he began. "She is an ornithologist from the states; that means she specializes in birds. Kate, this is Miguel Pereira. He is with Expedition Amazon, and he will accompany us on tour."

Miguel shook Kate's hand. "Doctor Beck," he said in heavily accented English. "Please call me Miguel."

"Call me Kate," she replied.

With introductions out of the way the men packed up the gear in the SUV and were soon tooling down the street in the direction of Expedition Amazon.

The trip from Manaus to the tour company was just over a hundred and fifty miles, so Kate settled in the back seat with her notebook and pen. The two men talked in the front seat, and she listened to them without interrupting. At first, they discussed the guide Rico, who had died at the hands of the creature they would be hunting. Then they began to talk about his pregnant wife, who had moved back in with family upon his death. According to Miguel, the woman was taking her husband's death very hard, and she had been bedridden since his funeral.

Eventually, the conversation turned to the trek they would be making, and Kate had her pen ready. She found that writing notes helped her to retain information, and it was a habit she practiced regularly. She was a firm believer in listening instead of speaking, particularly if one was trying to learn.

"I have assigned two guides to the tour," Miguel began. "I don't think you know either of them: Abilio Fonseca and Glaucio Duarte. Both of them were with other tours when we had the situation with you and

Rico."

Sam seemed suddenly very focused and all business. "They are aware of the circumstances and what we are all potentially facing?"

Miguel nodded. "Oh, yes. This is also the reason I am going as well, besides the fact that you asked me. I too took it a bit personally when we lost Rico. I feel a strong obligation to not only go but to look out for the men I am sending. When you asked me to accompany you, I had already planned to."

"So tell me about the men," Sam asked.

"Well," Miguel began, "Abilio has lived in the general area his entire life, and he has been a guide with us for the last seven years. Glaucio has been a guide with us for only three, but he worked with Amazonia Destino, or Amazon Destinations, for fifteen years. He lives and breathes the jungle."

Now Sam turned his body to face Miguel a bit better. "Have either of these men ever encountered the animal?"

Miguel's eyes were fastened securely on the road. "Glaucio claims to have heard stories, though he has never seen it with his eyes, and he has heard of no one dying. He did say that knowledge tells us that the bird is loud and violent. Abilio says he has heard nothing and has no experience with it, but when I told him what the tour was about, he was eager. Abilio has a bit of a reputation as a jungle soldier. Many request him for touring due to his level of courage."

"I would like to have a meeting before we head

out," Sam said. "It will be important to fill Dr. Beck in on safety and procedures."

Miguel nodded. "Yes," he replied. "We will want all introductions to be made thoroughly. It is important to know who you tour with."

The subject changed rather quickly after that, Kate noticed. The men began to talk about soccer, and the mood in the SUV lightened greatly, but as they neared the tour company, Miguel redirected the conversation back to the task at hand. He wanted the two of them to know what he was providing.

"I see that you have brought minimal gear, and that is good," Miguel stated matter-of-factly. "I have supplied tents and sleeping gear, which is already loaded into this car. The other vehicle will be carrying food and beverages, but it will be nothing fancy." He glanced at Kate out of the corner of his eye, then looked at Sam.

"I've filled Dr. Beck in very thoroughly on how it will be while we are out here," he replied. "This is a smart woman; she understands the need for less."

Suddenly Miguel turned the SUV into a driveway that led to a fairly large main lot. A building with a massive overhang stood in the central area of the property, and he steered the car beneath the overhang and parked there. Kate took notice of the words on the glass entrance:

Amazon Expedicao (Expedition Amazon)
Passeios na Selva (Jungle Tours)

Miguel turned his attention to Kate in the back seat. "You may leave your things here if you like; I will lock the car. We will only go in to have a brief meeting before leaving."

"Thank you," Kate replied. She kept her notebook and pen and climbed from the backseat.

The three of them closed the car doors, and Miguel activated the lock system. "Follow me," he said to them, then took the lead and headed into the building.

Sam walked next to Kate, who was busy taking it all in. She appeared confident and eager, but he could see that the newness of everything around her had her a bit overwhelmed.

"How are you feeling?" he asked.

She smiled at him. "Good. Just soaking it up."

He reached over and gave her shoulder a rub, which she appreciated. They went through the main reception area, where a man at a desk was speaking in Portuguese on the telephone. Miguel and the man nodded at each other before they passed through another door and walked down a long corridor. Finally, at the end of the hall, they entered a room which was obviously for conferences. There was a table with six chairs around it in the middle of the room. Up against one wall was a counter with a sink, coffee pot, cups, and condiments.

"Have a seat, Dr. Beck, Sam. Sit anyplace you like." Miguel sat at the head of the table. "Glaucio and Abilio will be in shortly. We are about ten minutes early."

The three of them sat mostly in silence as they waited. Kate turned to a clean page in her notebook, and at the top of it, she wrote the date, time, and a short heading that told her they had arrived at the tour headquarters. No sooner was she finished than the door to the conference room opened, and a man walked in.

Miguel stood up. "Sam, Dr. Beck, this is Glaucio Duarte. He will be one of the guides with us on this tour."

They shook hands all around, then Glaucio said in broken English, "Abilio coming."

The second guide appeared in less than a minute, and after the final introductions, the short meeting began. Miguel simply made it a point to make sure his men knew that this was Kate's maiden voyage into the jungle. Because of that fact, he wanted her to stick close by one of them at all times, preferably Sam, who readily agreed.

"Also to accommodate this, we will set up the camps for you; we have more experience and will get the task done quickly," he said. He turned his attention to Kate directly. "Dr. Beck, the jungle can be dangerous, and we are going to be in an area that is not often toured. Please do not wander off alone for any reason."

Kate agreed wholeheartedly, and she found that she was getting more and more nervous with each passing second. Sam must have noticed too because he made it a point to reach for her hand as Miguel spoke and gave it a squeeze. They smiled at each other, and it helped ease her mind a bit.

Next Miguel covered the reason for the tour with the guides. He had obviously already gone over things thoroughly with them, but he made a clear point that he could not be careful enough. He even showed them some photos of what Kate assumed was the site where Rico had been killed. She came to that conclusion by the look on Sam's face; the other men were speaking Portuguese, so she was left to guess.

By three o'clock they were ready to leave, and everyone seemed a bit amped. They piled into the SUVs: Miguel, Sam, and Kate in one, and Abilio and Glaucio in the other. Miguel drove the vehicle in the lead because he knew the way.

Kate sat in the back and tried to clear her mind for the adventure before her.

∞

Harold Kreiger and Roy Hastings checked into the Manaus Inn exhausted and dirty. Kreiger had opted for one of the cheapest hotels he could find, and he had insisted that they share a room. By the time they arrived, Hastings didn't have any more fight left in him. Kreiger had made him miserable for the last four days.

Once they were in the room, Hastings got in the shower while Kreiger began calling tour companies. He wanted to book an affordable tour, but for the time being, he just needed prices. He was going to have to contact the tour company Daniels and Beck were using and do some fast talking to find out exactly where they were touring, and then he would book an actual tour.

He also weighed out what exactly he should tell the guides. Certainly, they had heard about the 'bird,' as well as the death it had caused. Surely word got around in the business, and if that was the case, he didn't want to let on that he was basically 'stalking' another party. For all, he knew they had all been warned off. He hoped not; he had not come this far for nothing, and if it was the last thing he ever did he was going into that jungle on the heels of the competition.

The cheapest tour and the most willing, that he could find was a company with a tiny ad that should have told him what he was getting, but he didn't care. It was called Expedicao na Selva, or 'Jungle Expeditions.' Their prices were bottom of the barrel, and he let the receptionist know that he would be calling back with the proper tour information and complete the booking then.

Now it was time to call Expedition Amazon and begin fishing for information. Just as he was preparing to dial the number Hastings came out of the bathroom, dressed and toweling his hair. He looked revived, and Kreiger found himself longing for a shower as well.

"Any luck?" Hastings asked.

Kreiger sighed and sat back in his chair. "I found the most reasonable tour company. Now I'm going to get ahold of the one Beck and Daniels are using and try to worm their location out of someone."

Hastings tossed his wet towel on the floor by the door and began to comb his hair. "Well, I'm starving. I'm gonna go see what I can drum up. Do you want me to bring you anything?"

"Yeah, yes," Kreiger said. "Just bring me a serving of whatever you get. I'm gonna finish up here and shower."

"I'll see you in a bit then," the man replied as he left

the room.

Once the door was shut Kreiger turned his attention back to the task at hand. He thought over what he would say, and then quickly dialed the number to Expedition Amazon before he lost his nerve. It rang three times before it was answered.

"Estou sim?" greeted the man on the other end.

Kreiger had memorized the most important line of Portuguese he could think of: do you speak English. He had already had to use it when calling the other tour companies, and it appeared this call would be no exception.

"Voce fala ingles?"

"Yes, yes," came the response. "How we help you?"

"I am Dr. Jones from the United States," he began, treading very lightly with his approach. "Two of my associates are going on tour, and they are using your company. I was to meet them, but they gave me the wrong location, and I am using another company."

"Who you meeting?" the man asked.

Kreiger cleared his throat. "Dr. Kate Beck and photographer Samuel Daniels."

"Uno minute." Kreiger could hear paperwork being shuffled, but the man on the other end spoke to no one else, and that put him at ease. "They are going to a site not often on tours. Uh, papers say they enter at point four hundred thirteen."

"Four hundred thirteen?" Kreiger was jotting it down quickly, his heart beating faster at his luck.

"Yes, but this is not tour site," the man repeated.

"Only for experienced guides. Very dangerous. If you want I will wait for contact and let them know you're coming. They look for you that way."

But Kreiger had already hung up, leaving the man confused. He stared at the dead phone before shrugging and hanging up, and in only moments he forgot about Dr. Jones from the United States. Maybe they already knew he was coming. It was not his business.

Kreiger stood, smug and satisfied, and went into the bathroom to shower. As the hot water streamed down over his body, he laughed out loud. Obviously, they hadn't warned anyone about his intentions. Not a tour site? Dangerous? How dangerous could it be? After all, this incident was the only one of its kind. Kreiger put the warnings out of his mind and finished his shower.

By the time Hastings returned with his food he had already called Jungle Expeditions back and booked a tour, with a single guide, to point four hundred thirteen. The guide would pick them up at the entrance to the Inn at eight in the morning, giving them plenty of time to rest. The company would also supply food, water, and sleeping bags for the next three days, and all at a low, low bargain price.

Things were finally starting to go Harold Kreiger's way.

CHAPTER 16

The two SUVs made their way up the narrow trail, with trees hanging over like so much protective roofing. While it was hot and the air felt wet, the trees provided much-needed shade, and it didn't take Kate long to thank her lucky stars for the protection. Even though the trail was shadowy, she was able to enjoy the plants and wildlife and was even treated to a breathtaking waterfall during the first half-hour of the drive.

Sam and Miguel were talking in the front seat, and she made it a point only to listen. Most of what they said was in Portuguese, she assumed to make it easier on Miguel. By the way, they were pointing and the tones their voices took on she figured they were talking about that fateful day the 'bird' first came into their lives.

After a while longer, Sam sat forward in his seat and began to concentrate on the road before them. In English, he said, "The screaming started right about here, I think." After only a minute more he said, "Yes! Yes, Miguel. This was it."

Miguel pulled off to the side, which really didn't mean much due to the narrowness of the trail. Kate glanced out the back and saw that the other SUV was following suit. Miguel cut the engine, and they all sat in silence.

After a bit, the driver turned to Sam. "Do we want to set up camp here, or do you want to go in further?"

Sam thought it over. "Maybe just a bit further. You have weapons? Protection?"

Miguel nodded as he stared out the window at the surrounding jungle. "Both guns and dart guns. We know it is important to keep the thing alive. They have a large cage in the cargo space in the back of their car, and they have guns as well. We should be good if we are careful."

He started the car again and then rolled his window down and motioned to the men behind him with his arm. They started moving again, and this time they drove for about ten minutes before Miguel slowed to a stop at a much wider section of trail. He put the vehicle in park and turned to Sam.

"This is a good place for parking," he said, "and see the clearing off to the right here? Perfect for camp. Water nearby."

Kate took immediate notice of a small waterfall that was close to the clearing and emptied into a clear stream. The beauty of it all brought a smile to her face. She couldn't believe she was here.

Sam turned to Kate in the back seat and touched her knee to get her attention. "How are you?"

She turned to him, a smile glued to her face. "Wonderful," she said. "Just one thing: I don't know that I should camp alone, with it being my first time and all."

"No worries," he told her. "We will share a two-man tent. Are you okay with that?" She nodded, then Sam said, "You should stay in here, just until we set up camp. Once that is done we will venture out a bit before nightfall, but not for too long. Just hang out, okay?"

The men set about setting up camp while Kate sat in the back of the SUV and did a full three-sixty, taking in everything around her and around the site. She had never experienced such beauty, and the sounds of the animals were unbelievable. She couldn't wait to start hiking.

The camp was done in record time, and soon Abilio came over to the SUV and opened Kate's door. "Mister says you can come now if you're ready." He smiled at her nervously, and she could tell he was careful not to make her nervous. She nodded eagerly and handed the bag that held her and Sam's stuff to the man; he took it with a nod and stood back to give her room to get out.

She put her things in the tent that Sam pointed to, then came out with a small recording device. She knew it would work much better than trying to take notes, and she could transcribe everything later. Glaucio passed out bottles of water with condensation on the side, and she immediately took a sip; she realized she was very thirsty, and even a small sip was refreshing.

"Okay," Miguel began as he pointed toward the east. "We will set off in that direction first, but we will not go too far. Mr. Daniels says that is the direction the animal came from."

"It screamed a couple of times, very loudly, before it reached us," Sam said. "It sounded like a woman screaming."

Miguel repeated Sam's words in Portuguese to the two guides, who nodded at him as he spoke. He then turned back to Sam and Kate. "Okay, we go now."

They began to walk, and Kate noticed a very specific order to the line they walked in. Miguel led the way; behind him was Glaucio, then Kate, Sam, and finally Abilio. The two guides and Miguel had guns on their hips and tranquilizer guns in their hands. Kate felt no fear, and the sound of the animals and birds around them made her feel welcome.

The group ended up walking in a small circle around the place they would be camping. Kate concluded this was to ensure the safety of the site and make sure they were familiar with the general surroundings. By the time they were done the shadows were deepening, and Miguel finally suggested they return, build a fire and eat, and then relax a bit before turning in.

"Tomorrow will be an important day for walking," he said as he observed the area. "Do not want to tire before we start."

They turned around this time Miguel pulling up the rear and headed back to camp. It had been unexciting, if not a disappointing first day, but Kate had a feeling they would all be getting plenty of excitement soon enough. Best to take it a small step at a time.

∞

Kreiger and Hastings ended up visiting a small bar

down the block from the Inn before they retired for the night. They both had a couple of brandies and took in the people and surroundings, then they made their way back to the room. Neither of them thought it wise to face the following day hung over or too tired.

As Kreiger lay in the double bed with Hastings snoring loudly next to him, he mentally planned his morning. They would rise and check out around six thirty or seven, at the latest. The guide from Expedicao na Selva would pick them up at eight, and then they would drive for a couple of hours directly to area four hundred thirteen; they would be there by ten.

Finally, he dozed off, and he dreamed of giving acceptance speeches and lectures for his findings. In his dreams he was invincible, and he was living at the top of his game. He finally had everything he ever wanted, and he didn't even care who paid for it all.

R.W.K. Clark

CHAPTER 17

The small fire burned surprisingly bright, at least in Kate's opinion. She sat content at the opening of the tent which Sam and she would use, and she tried to keep up with the conversation they were having, which was partially in English and partially in Portuguese. Eventually, she gave up and hooked her earbuds up to her small recorder to transcribe what little had taken place during their short hike around the campsite.

They had eaten cold sandwiches from a cooler and drunk chilled water, both of which Kate found to be very satisfying. Her belly was full, and she was happy to be listening to the recording she had made because as soon as it was finished, she intended to lie down and get some rest. It ended up taking her only about a half-hour, and it took that long only because she was so obsessive when it came to notes.

She put her things inside her tent, then went back out to find a place to relieve herself. As she stood, Sam looked up at her. He was trying to read her mind, so she didn't have to speak out loud, but she didn't mind.

"Just going to go to the bathroom, then I'm turning in, I think," she told him.

He grabbed a flashlight from next to his leg and stood. "Do you want me to go with you?"

She nodded. "It's pretty dark, and it won't take me but a minute. Thank you."

"No problem," he replied, and he led her behind their tent and into some foliage. She took care of her business and was extremely relieved when he reached through the leaves with a roll of toilet tissue.

"Oh, I was just about ready to panic," she laughed. She took it from Sam, who was laughing as well. "Very funny, Sam."

"Yeah, well, you can count on me."

They soon headed back to the camp, and Kate went inside the tent and curled up in her sleeping bag. The men respectfully kept their voices down so she could sleep, but her excitement kept her from dozing off too quickly. She found herself thinking about the bird, and wondering if they would be so lucky as to track it down. It consumed her waking thoughts until sleep won, and she finally began to dream.

∞

Suddenly a woman screamed, and she screamed loudly, as though she were being murdered.

Kate sat up immediately, at full attention and frozen in place. The men were suddenly silent outside the tent, and she strained to hear anything she could, but no sound of any kind came. At one point she heard one of the men 'shush' the others, and she could make out their frozen shadows through the canvas of her tent, guns in hand.

The scream came again, this time louder, closer, and more desperate-sounding than before. A chill broke out over her entire body, and for the first time since they had set off on this adventure, she was frightened. Her blood ran cold in her veins.

Through the canvas, a new shadow came, and it came all at once. It landed on what she thought was a small circular table made of aluminum, and it was about five feet from the fire on the opposing side from her tent. Sam and Miguel had been seated to the right and Glaucio and Abilio to the left. She could make out the shadows of all four men and their weapons, but this shadow was not the shadow of any man; it was the shadow of what appeared to be a massive bird.

Kate held her breath, scared to death that the thing would see or hear her in the firelight and the silence of the jungle. Beads of sweat broke out on her forehead, and she realized she was utterly petrified.

She heard Sam speak then, in a voice that was just above a whisper. "Stay in there, Kate. Don't move."

Abilio, who was seated closest to her tent on the right, was slowly lifting his tranquilizer gun. The animal abruptly caught the movement and turned toward him, which prompted Miguel and Glaucio to do the same. The bird took notice of all of it, its large head swinging back and forth with each of their movements.

Sam spoke again, this time his voice a bit more insistent. "Don't look in its eyes, men. Don't look it in the eye."

The bird gave another scream, its head flung back

and its mouth wide. Gosh, how Kate wished she could see it. Why did she come if she couldn't observe? What had been the point?

She leaned forward and unzipped the door to the tent very slowly, and the bird didn't miss the movement. It turned to face her, its head and body clear in the firelight, and Kate got a good look before her senses took over. She mustn't look it in the eye! Quickly she crouched down and let her hand fall from the zipper.

Next came a sound like a loud 'zip!' followed by a whine. The bird gave another scream, and then in a storm of beating feathers, it took flight. It continued to beat its feathers as it hovered over the camp for a brief moment, uttered a final scream, and took off into the night.

"I missed!" It was the voice of Glaucio. He had attempted to tranquilize the animal, but his shaking, frightened hand had missed. "I'm sorry! I miss!"

The men were all standing now, their guns in the air waving, flashlights blazing. Kate unzipped her tent another foot and took notice of Sam, who also seemed to be carrying a weapon. They were all turning around in circles and trying to see the animal once again.

After about ten minutes of rushing chaos, Miguel spoke. "It has gone, men. I believe it has gone."

The ruckus began to die down, but Kate could tell that the men were on edge. Miguel continued, "We will take shifts this night. It is not safe for all of us to sleep at the same time." He turned to the two guides. "Sam and I will go to one o'clock in the morning. You two will take over and go to five. We will then head out. It went in that direction as far as I could tell."

Sam agreed. "It was the same way it went last time: east."

It took about twenty minutes before the men were calm enough to begin carrying out the plan for the night. Once they were a little calm, the two guides went to their tent and turned in. Kate observed them looking over their shoulders the entire time until they were safely zipped up inside. Sam crouched down next to Kate just inside their tent.

"Are you okay?" he asked.

She nodded. "I wish you hadn't have tried to open the tent," he continued.

"If I am not here to study, to help, then why did I come? Maybe you should show me how to use one of those damn guns, so I'm not so helpless," she said with a defiant shake of her head. "I'm a scientist, Sam. What did you expect?"

Sam turned and looked at Miguel, who glanced at him and offered a shrug before turning his attention back to the night and his vigil. He turned back to Kate then. "As I am sure you heard I am going to take the first watch with Miguel. Try to get some sleep. I'll wake you at one, when we change shifts, okay?"

He leaned inside and kissed her on the mouth, and she returned the gesture before leaning back and saying, "It was beautiful, Sam."

He nodded and breathed a heavy sigh. "That's the problem," he replied.

Kate tossed and turned and managed to get very little sleep. What sleep she did get was filled with the bird's screams, and more than once she was startled awake by the sounds that filled her own head. When Sam woke her at ten after one to tell her he was there, she wrapped her arms around him and clung to him.

"Are you going to be okay?" he asked yet again as they settled in.

"Mmm-hmmm," she replied.

He curled his fingers around hers and continued. "In the morning, before we head out, we will find a spot near the water so you can freshen up if you want; the days here can get very sticky."

She didn't reply; she was already feeling safer, and sleep came much easier this time. There were no more screams in her dreams, and there was no more chaos from outside the tent. It seemed that the animal had been frightened off, but everyone hoped it wasn't for good. Even Miguel, Glaucio, and Abilio were set on finding the thing now, and figuring out how to subdue it.

Sam himself was obsessed. He tried to sleep, but rest came hard. The last conscious thought he had before drifting was, "I hope it is the only one. I hope there are no more." With that Sam Daniels began to finally dream.

CHAPTER 18

Kate was awakened by the sounds of the jungle: the birds, the insects, and the nearby waterfall. At first, right after her eyes fluttered open, she simply lay there, still and smiling, but then she recalled the creature, beautiful and terrifying. She recalled its scream and its determination, and she sat up straight in her sleeping bag, her heart pounding. The bag next to hers was empty; where was Sam?

As soon as the thought crossed her mind, she heard his voice, speaking in low tones outside the tent. "I'm going to wake Dr. Beck with this coffee. I want to give her time to visit the water if she wants, and get her wits about her." No sooner had he spoken the words than the zipper on the tent slowly came down.

"Good morning." Sam smiled as he poked a metal cup filled with hot black liquid through the opening. "I seem to recall that you take it with cream."

Kate smiled and reached out for the cup gratefully. "Thank you, and good morning yourself."

"The others have all been up; I don't think any of us really got any good rest last night," Sam said with a shrug. "These guys are troopers, though, and the strong coffee doesn't hurt. Take a few minutes to get woken up if you like, then we can walk to the water."

Kate sipped the coffee and winced at its potency. "Wow," she said. "It won't take long, I'm pretty sure. Not with this stuff."

Sam chuckled and rocked back on his ankles, then zipped the tent back up. Kate took another drink of the coffee before setting the cup down and holding her hand up to it in surrender. She fished through the bag that she was sharing with Sam and found a small makeup bag that held a travel toothbrush, paste, and a small hairbrush. That would be all she needed. Once she had her shoes on, she grabbed the cup as well and made her way from the tent.

The four men already had their tents down and packed, and all of their other gear was organized neatly, ready for them to move. "I'm ready if you are, Sam. Should I fold up the sleeping bags first?"

"No," he replied. "The guys will take care of that. Follow me."

Kate followed Sam as he led her between beautiful green plants and through thickets with massive leaves. They wove around a bit, but in a short time, they were at the water, the waterfall pouring beautifully over the rocks nearby. Kate was breathless at the beautiful sight, then realized that the sound of the water made her have to go to the bathroom desperately.

"Oh, dang, Sam, I forgot…," she began.

Sam turned to her and smiled, holding a partial roll of toilet tissue out to her. "I didn't."

"Wow, I don't know what I would do without you." She took the roll and held out her makeup bag for him to hold. "I'll be right back."

He smiled and turned to gaze at the water. "Take your time."

Kate found a private spot in the greenery only about six feet away. She was able to relieve herself quickly and made sure to gather the paper she used, wrapping it inside more of the same. When she got back to Sam, he stood holding out her makeup bag.

"There's a spot where you can reach the water fairly easily without falling in," he said, pointing to a level piece of ground at the water's edge. Kate took her things and walked down easily.

It took her only ten minutes to brush her teeth, wash her face, and run the brush through her hair. She put a ponytail holder in, packed her things, and went back to Sam. He approached her and took her face in his hands. He looked in her eyes for a moment before pressing his lips against hers. He seemed to do so tentatively, so Kate took the upper hand. She dropped her small bag to the ground, put her hands in his hair, and pulled him to her. Her tongue found his quickly, and she pressed her body against his hungrily.

Sam pulled back and smiled, then turned and looked back in the direction of their camp. They could hear the voices of Miguel and the guides, but the plant life provided them with very private space. He turned back to her to see her smiling at him.

"Looks like a perfect opportunity to me," she

whispered.

Sam's left hand went to her breast, which he squeezed gently as he stroked her nipple with his thumb. Kate wasted no time, either. Her hands both went to his belt, which she had unbuckled in seconds flat. Her hand found its way down the front of his pants and his briefs to find he was already rock-hard, so she stroked him as her tongue darted around in his mouth.

The two of them continued groping and kissing as Sam began to lower her to the ground. She stopped him only long enough to take her own pants off one leg. She parted them for him then, and after teasing her with his erection for only a moment, he thrust it inside of her, then slowed to make it last longer than thirty seconds.

They moved together, their lips locked, without making a sound. After only a minute Kate's movements became more and more feverish. She pulled away from his mouth and looked him in the eye. "I'm going to come," she whispered. Her eyes closed, and she could feel the ground beneath her bare bottom as she came. Her body stiffened and pressed against him urgently, and that was all it took for Sam. He buried himself deep inside her with one final thrust, letting go of all he had been trying to hold back.

They lay on the ground recuperating for only a brief moment before they heard Miguel. "We are nearly ready, Mr. Daniels!"

Sam looked at her, and they began to giggle. Finally, they pulled apart, and Kate said, "I'm going to go to the bathroom again." She grabbed the toilet paper and ducked back into the oversized leaves. When she returned, all put together, Sam had righted himself as well. Kate found her bag on the ground, gave her hand to Sam, and with broad smiles they made their way back to the camp.

"So, what's the plan?" She asked as they walked.

"East," he replied. "We are heading due east, just like the bird. When Miguel and I pulled our shift, we heard a couple more screams. They were distant, but both of us agreed they came directly from the east."

Kate nodded. "Sounds good. What time is it?"

"Actually it is probably six by now. We wanted the guides to get an extra half-hour's sleep, so we didn't wake them until five thirty, but they were already up."

They got back to the camp, and the men grabbed up the gear. "We are all ready, yes?" Miguel had a smile on his face, and if Kate wasn't mistaken, he had an eager look in his eye. He turned his attention to her and handed her what appeared to be an energy bar. "Breakfast for the lady. Eat it when you want."

They lined up in the same order as the day before and began their trek. Kate had a feeling about the day: it was a mixture of dread and excitement. She only hoped that the 'dread' wasn't some kind of terrible omen.

∞

Harold Kreiger and Roy Hastings were riding along in a large truck; their guide had picked them up about fifteen minutes early, and Kreiger had been pleased. He had difficulty sleeping all night, and by the time he had gotten out of bed, dressed, and woke Hastings he had been ready to head out, and it had been only six thirty.

They drove until ten thirty, at which time they came to the marker reading '413'. A very narrow trail veered off at that spot. Their guide, a man of about twenty-six by the name of Marcario Araullo, seemed to know his way around and was eager to please, though Kreiger didn't have any idea how much experience he really had. As a matter of fact, the question never even crossed the paleontologist's mind.

They didn't really talk, though the guide did speak in broken English fairly well. After he turned on 413 and got the truck going on the trail, he turned to Kreiger. "Where now, mister?"

"Uh, just keep going until we see my associates, um, my partners," Kreiger said, looking at the man out of the corner of his eye. "They will be on the trail somewhere. They set out yesterday."

The guide nodded at him, and they continued to drive. After about a half-hour they came upon two SUVs. Both of them were marked with 'Expedition Amazon' on the front doors, and though they were pulled to the side of the trail, there was little room for the truck to get around.

"Stop. I want to make sure this is them," Kreiger said. The guide brought the truck to a halt, and Kreiger climbed from the passenger side and walked up to the vehicles. He put his hand on the hood of the one in front: it was cold, as was the second.

Marcario rolled down the driver's window and leaned out. "They might be far ahead, mister sir," he said. "If they are hiking they would park and camp elsewhere. See," the man pointed at a nearby clearing. In the middle were the remains of a fire, the smoke trickling skyward. "They camp there, I bet."

Kreiger made his way to the clearing. The fire was nothing more than a bit of rubble, the smoke a fading memory. He could see where tents had likely been: three of them, to be exact. There were other telltale signs as well. From what Kreiger saw he would guess they had been gone three or four hours, maybe more.

He returned to the truck and noticed that Hastings was sleeping in the back, his mouth wide open. Kreiger shook his head in disgust and climbed back into his seat. "If they left early, say around six in the morning, how far would they be, do you think?" he asked the guide.

Marcario shrugged. "If they are going fast, they probably would be an hour by car. If slow, thirty or forty-five minutes. We can drive and look as we go. They are probably not too far off the path."

Kreiger buckled his seat belt. "Let's go then, man!" Marcario quickly put the truck in gear and then pulled away.

Well, he had found their camp; at least, he was willing to bet that it was. He knew from the notes stolen from Jason Seward that it was the site where the creature was first seen. It was off the beaten path and not normally visited during expeditions. According to what Sam Daniels had told him, his deceased guide had told him it was a secret spot, so he was sure that was their camp from the night before. They were close; he could almost smell them.

They made their way slowly around the two SUVs and then picked up their speed a bit. Soon they would find their group and Kreiger would attempt to follow them on the sly. He would tell Marcario to keep his mouth shut and do what he said, to lead him like he was being paid to do, and help him track the group.

It would be too easy.

CHAPTER 19

By eleven o'clock Sam, Kate, and the other men had worked up a bit of an appetite. Sam knew that the men would all be fine, but it was Kate he was worried about. He took it up with Miguel as they walked.

"Do you want to stop so we can have a quick bite? An early lunch?"

Miguel stopped their trek and looked around. "No good spots right here, but I am sure we will soon find one. Let's walk a bit more, make a clearing. I have some canned soup in my pack, enough for all, large cans. We can build a small fire and eat warm food. Better for good energy."

Sam nodded at him and asked Kate, "Are you good for now?"

She had waited to eat her energy bar until nine thirty so she would manage. She nodded at him, and the group set off once again. They didn't have to walk far; they came to the perfect spot, a small clearing surrounded by rocks, only ten minutes further along.

Kate crept off to relieve herself while the men built a small fire for cooking. It took her only a moment, and she was fastening her pants when she heard a car. It was enough of a surprise to cause her to stop what she was doing right away and look around. She saw nothing, but the sound seemed to get louder. Kate finally got her pants fastened and quickly made her way back to the men.

As she approached the clearing, the vehicle stopped. She could see it then, or at least the hood of the car. It appeared to be a beige colored truck. A car door slammed then, and she heard Miguel's voice clearly.

"Someone is here with us, Mr. Daniels."

Kate picked up her pace and headed toward the men. Just as she stepped into the clearing, Harold Kreiger appeared, stepping out from behind some leaves. He had a surprised look on his face as if he didn't expect them to be directly on the other side of the greenery.

"What the heck, Harold?" Kate was furious. The so-and-so jerk had used Jason's notes to track them down! She turned on her heel and strode toward him, livid with anger. No one was as surprised as Kreiger when Kate reached him, drew back, and slapped him hard across the face.

"How dare you? How dare you go this far?" She was so angry she was shaking.

Kreiger's hand went up to his cheek and stroked it. Kate looked at the men, and they were all standing. Both guides had their guns out and aimed, and Sam and Miguel looked like they were ready to fight.

Suddenly the paleontologist broke out in laughter. "I would say this is fair game at this point, wouldn't you,

Dr. Beck?"

Kate could do nothing but shake her head in disgust. Her mind raced as she considered her words. Finally, she said to him, "Do what you will, Dr. Kreiger. I am going to see to it that you lose your position with the university. Once that is done nothing you may or may not accomplish here will be worth crap."

Kreiger laughed again. "It's not like I am asking you to let me join you, now is it?"

"It would have been more polite for you to ask than to do things the way you have done them thus far," she replied. She turned to Sam. "I say we let him go on ahead. Let him see if he can find it since he seems to know so much."

Sam shook his head, a look of wonder in his eyes. "Kate, we've come so far…"

"Yes, Kate," Kreiger said, smiling as he rubbed his red cheek. "It's only fair for me to let you continue to lead the way."

Two more car doors slammed, and soon Roy Hastings and a man in guide khakis appeared out of the greenery behind Kreiger. Hastings had a frightened look on his face as if all this was more than he had bargained for. The other man simply looked confused.

"We are not going to lead you anywhere," Kate said, her voice dangerously shrill.

Kreiger removed the hat he was wearing from his head and looked at the sky and leaves above. "Well," he said, "It seems you and your party are heading due east. I can only assume you know the right way." He looked at Kate, a sly smile on his face. "Have you seen it yet?"

As if on cue, a deafening scream filled the air around them. Everyone froze except for Miguel, who took his tranquilizer gun from his belt and began to search the sky around them with his eyes. The other two men, Abilio and Glaucio, kept their handguns poised as they too scanned their surroundings. Kreiger's eyes lit up as he took note of their reaction; Hastings looked as if he might piss himself.

The scream came again, closer now, and suddenly a rush of wings filled their ears. Then, on a young kapok tree that had been broken nearby, the creature lit. Its claws took hold with an audible sound, and as it settled, it offered yet another ear-piercing screech.

All of the men in Kate and Sam's party, including Sam himself, had either handguns or tranquilizer guns ready. "Don't look at it," Sam said. "Not in the eyes."

Kate kept her eyes off the creature as she held her position carefully. She had no intention of drawing any kind of attention to herself through movement, but Hastings fainted dead away and fell to the ground. Kate shifted her eyes from Hastings to the young tour guide, whose eyes were wide with wonder as he gazed at the beautiful creature.

"Don't look at its eyes," she whispered to the man, but he took no notice of her words. She glanced at Kreiger and saw that he, too, was staring directly at the animal.

"I've never," he stammered, "I've never seen anything like it."

The young guide took a step forward as if to approach the creature, but Kate put her arm out instinctively. "No!" she hissed. The man didn't seem to take notice of her at all, but he did stop in his tracks. It didn't matter anymore; Kreiger was hooked, and it looked like the animal was just as preoccupied with the paleontologist.

He stared at it, his heart racing. Without looking away, Kreiger said, "See? I won't need your guidance any further. You have led me right to it."

He took a step toward the bird, staring and smiling. The bird began to make a sing-song sound in its throat, almost like musical gargling. Kreiger took yet another step.

"How do you intend to capture it, Harold?" Kate was afraid for the man. She knew in her heart that he was a goner, just the way Sam had told her Rico had been. "Kreiger, think about what you are doing!"

Miguel, Sam, and their two guides simply watched as Kreiger neared the animal, which almost seemed to begin smiling. It was paying no mind to anyone else, only the stupid, self-indulgent scientist that approached it.

When Kreiger was about four feet from it, Sam finally spoke. "Dr. Kreiger, you are in a bad way, man."

He chuckled in response and closed the gap between himself and the creature. Now he stood only a foot in front of it. The thing continued to sing its bizarre song while it held Kreiger's eyes. It tilted its head to the left, then to the right. Kreiger's hands came up as if he were going to pet or caress the thing, but his hands never finished their journey.

The thing sat on the fallen trunk of the kapok at about chest level with Dr. Kreiger. Suddenly its left 'hand' shot out and grasped the man painfully by the right shoulder. The talon-like growths at the tips of the phalanges tore through his shirt like it were soft butter, and soon blood flowered through the white cotton fabric. Its right 'hand' grabbed onto his face with great strength, tearing at the flesh and turning it into rags. Kreiger opened his mouth and screamed, but the animal could have cared less about his crying. Just as Sam had described, it then stabbed out the man's eyes with two rapid thrusts of its beak, and it spread its wings and lifted off, dangling the kicking and screaming man beneath it.

It opened its mouth then and uttered yet another scream, this one louder for the close proximity. Kate's hands went to her ears, and she winced with pain. Out of the corner of her eye, she saw the leaves of the greenery which Kreiger had come through move again, and she turned in their direction. The young guide was gone. He had taken off running toward the truck in terror, leaving his two charges to fend for themselves. She heard the engine start and vaguely registered the tires peeling out on the jungle floor, then the engine faded in the distance.

The creature hovered in the air with Kreiger, its continued scream seeming to last an eternity. Blood dripped from the man in large trails and dropped to the ground in large splashes. Kreiger was only twitching now, and Kate knew he was probably in shock. It didn't matter; he was as good as dead.

Then, as quickly as it arrived, the thing took to the sky, avoiding the trees and overhead leaves with great grace and skill. Sam and Miguel seemed to snap out of their own reverie then, and they brought the tranquilizer guns up and fired both. The target was missed, and it faded into the sky as it flew away from the group.

Behind her, Kate heard whimpering. She turned around to see Hastings sitting on the jungle floor, shaking like a leaf. "What?" She went to him and knelt beside him. As soon as she touched him to comfort him, he broke down like a small child, weeping and heaving with great sobs.

She turned her attention to Sam and shook her head. Sam simply watched her for a moment, then turned to Miguel. "We have to catch it. We have to catch it and stop it," he said quietly.

Miguel nodded and continued to look at the now empty sky. "Yes. Stop it we must."

∞

It flew high above the trees, soaring, almost seeming to dance in the wind. Its prey was gripped tightly in its powerful phalanges; it had stopped struggling long ago. It would take its meal to its nest and dine on its blood. Until it reached the nest, it would dance in the wind as it flew.

After fifteen minutes it came to a massive kapok tree that towered above all the rest. There, nestled at the top, was a giant nest made of leaves, dirt, and other chunks of debris. The nest was as big as a small studio apartment, and it provided the creature with all the room it needed.

It hovered over the top of its home, aiming, then dropped the man dead center. As soon as Kreiger hit the nest, he woke; he had only fainted in its grasp. He couldn't see, and suddenly the memory of what happened to him flooded his mind. His flesh burned and bled, as did his eyes, or what was left of them.

Kreiger screamed and began to scramble around. The creature sat on the edge of its nest and watched its prey cry and struggle blindly. It was entertained and even seemed to smile as it watched the show.

The prey screamed and sobbed, crawling on its hands and knees, looking for any way out of the trouble it was in. The creature let it do what it would, but only for a short time. Soon, the rumbling in its stomach was louder than the screams of its food, and it dove, driving its razor-sharp beak through the man's back. It came out the other side, and blood flowed with it like a faucet had been turned on.

Kreiger's body jerked once, twice, three times. Suddenly his screaming stopped, and he went limp. The creature withdrew its beak and watched as its prey collapsed on the floor of the nest. Its pink tongue came out and tasted the blood, then it charged and covered the dead man. Dr. Harold Kreiger had found what he had come looking for.

CHAPTER 20

Kate couldn't believe what she had witnessed.

She sat next to the water on a rock, her elbows on her knees and her chin in her hands. She seemed frozen emotionally, mostly to herself. She was amazed at the lack of compassion she felt for her one-time colleague.

It was because he had asked for it; Kreiger had asked for it.

She turned around and watched as the guides set up camp. It was nearly seven in the evening, and they were not willing to travel at night at all in light of the incident with the creature. Hastings was sitting on the ground staring at the fire that had been built. She was pretty sure that man would never be the same again. He had always been a bit weak.

She turned back to the water and reached down to swish her finger in it. It was amazingly clear, and she could see the rocks at the bottom almost as if there were no water at all. It was also chilled nicely, and she imagined that it tasted heavenly.

She pulled up the picture of Kreiger dangling in the creature's grasp once again, but now she wasn't thinking about the dead paleontologist; she was thinking about the animal that had killed him. It certainly looked like a bird, with its stunning feathers and sharp beak. But that forsaken thing was not a bird. After observing it at work she was sure of that, and she found herself wishing she had studied dinosaurs after all.

It was brutal in its violence, and it killed with purpose and intent. There was an intelligence in its eyes that seemed matched only by humans. She was certain that, aside from their design, that was why the creature's eyes looked so… human. It… knew.

"How are you doing, Kate?" Sam had crept up silently behind her, but even the surprise of his voice didn't faze her. She doubted much would ever faze her again.

She turned to him and smiled. "I'm as good as can be expected, I guess."

Sam sat down next to her on the ground and rubbed her back with his hand. "I'm sorry you had to see that."

"It was just like you said," she replied, focusing her attention back on the clean water.

Sam grunted. "Unfortunately. I could go the rest of my life without ever seeing that again."

Kate turned to him and smiled. "Me too."

They were quiet for only a minute before Sam spoke. "What do you think it is, Kate?"

"Well," she began, "I think Kreiger was right. I think it is likely a dinosaur or relation to one. I think birds may have evolved from it, possibly. Anyway, it's impossible to really know without capturing it and studying it. I really want it alive, but after today I am willing to compromise."

They laughed at her joke, but they both knew that if the thing had to be killed, then it would be so. They sat in silence for a moment, and Kate reached out and took Sam's hand. He squeezed it in return, and they continued in their silence.

After a while, he asked, "Do you want to walk along the water?"

Kate looked up and down the shore a bit, then smiled and nodded. "I think I would like that," she replied.

They stood and held hands as they made their way along the water's edge. There was no need for words; the things they left unsaid were speaking loudly enough. After about ten minutes Kate turned around and looked toward the camp. She could see the smoke from the fire, but the camp itself was blocked by plant life. Then she looked down at Sam's belt, and when she saw he was armed, she breathed a sigh of relief.

"I want to swim," she said simply.

They stopped, and Sam looked at the water. "Well, why don't you take a dip?" he asked her.

"Why don't you take a dip with me?"

Sam's eyes went to the sky and his mind to the creature. There had been no screams since it took off, and it likely had its belly full now. He looked down at the handgun, then the tranquilizer gun, both of which were on his belt. He took the handgun from its holster and nodded. "Okay, then. I think I will."

The pair got naked in no time, and they were soon

in the crisp, clear water. Kate wanted to stay closer to shore, and Sam agreed. He thought that they were likely safer in the water than on land, but he had his gun, so it didn't matter. He kept the gun above water, and the two of them bobbed up and down, talking about Hastings.

"He's dead weight," Sam was saying. "I hope we find this thing and get out of here soon. The guy seems to have snapped."

Kate treaded water moving toward him as he spoke. She put her arms around his neck and wrapped her legs around his waist, then planted her lips firmly on his. She knew what she needed was a stress reliever, and Sam sure seemed to fit the bill.

He responded eagerly to her kisses, and she pressed her crotch against him so she could feel his growing erection. Kate rubbed herself against it, moaning as she kissed him. He took his free hand and held her head against his, then let it wander beneath the water. He wanted to feel her; he wanted his hand between her legs.

Kate read his mind and backed off slightly, giving his hand the room it needed. He found the spot he was looking for and gently stroked, getting a rhythm. Now she stopped kissing him and rested her head on his shoulder. She closed her eyes and let herself be overcome by the pleasure, and Sam was certainly giving her a lot of it.

He continued to stroke and then slipped his finger inside of her. She groaned out loud, her muscles clenching around his finger as it went in and out, in and out. He removed it then and began stroking her again.

"Oh, it's going to happen!" Her hips began to rock against his hand rhythmically, and when she came, she cried out.

Sam pushed himself into her right then, and she continued to rock on him, up and down, in and out. He came with force, his entire body going rigid. He put his mouth on hers to keep himself from crying out as well, and she thrust her tongue against his. They held each other tightly as they rode out the orgasms until finally, they let out great breaths of relief.

The two of them began laughing. They listened for the others, but all they could hear were their voices, which were at the campsite. Kate and Sam smiled at each other.

"I think I love you, Kate Beck," Sam said, his smile fading and his face serious.

She grew serious as well. "Ditto, Sam Daniels."

They kissed one more time, and as if they were reading each other's minds they separated and headed for the shore. Sam was still holding the gun up, which made Kate laugh. She couldn't believe he had done it.

"Is your arm asleep?" she teased.

He grinned. "I don't know. I can't feel it."

They climbed from the water and dressed quickly, then made their way back to camp. Both of them had wet hair which was soaking the collars of their shirts, but neither cared what anyone thought. It was what it was.

Miguel looked up when they approached and gave Sam a grin. "I was about to come looking for you, Mr.

Daniels, but then I thought better of it."

"Don't come looking for me unless you hear screaming, and I mean the bird kind," Sam replied sarcastically.

The men chuckled, and Kate shook her head and tried to hide her blushing cheeks. Glaucio and Abilio were cooking the cans of soup that they never got to eat at lunch, and it smelled wonderful. Kate's stomach growled fiercely; it was definitely time to get some nourishment. She then remembered the takeout they had ordered before they left Manaus.

"Sam, we still have that food in our bag from the hotel," she said.

"Ugh!" Sam replied. "You may as well throw it in the fire."

She picked up their bag, which was placed outside the tent they would sleep in, and fished through it. At the bottom, she found the bag with the wrapped items, and she took them to the fire and put them in. She saw the soup bubbling and steaming, and she said to Glaucio, "It smells so good."

The man smiled and nodded at her. "You are hungry, yes?"

"Very!"

Miguel joined the conversation. "We all are, but it is a surprise we can eat after what happened earlier." He sat near the others, and Sam joined them. Abilio served the soup, including a bowl for Hastings. He was curled up in Miguel's open tent. The man glanced at the traumatized paleontologist, then turned to Kate and

Sam. "They are the ones who wanted to… steal… the bird from you?"

"Well," Sam began, "they wanted the credit for finding a creature no one has seen before. They wanted fame and fortune."

Miguel grunted. "Well, the other one may not have gotten his fortune, but he may have a bit of fame. As a victim."

The group fell silent as they accepted their food and began to eat. They were all ravenous, and it showed in the way they focused so intently on the food before them. Kate rose about halfway through and fetched bottles of water to pass out, but that was the only interruption in the meal.

∞

When they were done eating Kate took it upon herself to wash their dishes and utensils. She dried them and arranged them in the kit they belonged in, then returned to the fire. On the way, she noticed that Hastings had not touched his dinner; it sat at his feet, and he still lay in the fetal position inside Miguel's tent.

Kate knelt down at the opening. "Roy, are you going to eat?" she asked him. "You have to keep up your strength, you know."

His eyes were open, and he glanced at her. "I've never seen anything like that, Kate." His voice was low, and it shook as he spoke.

She made herself more comfortable on the ground and reached inside the tent to pat the man on the leg. "I know, Roy. It was a first for me, too."

"Where did it take him, Kate?"

She shrugged. She hadn't really thought about it and didn't want to, but now Hastings wanted to finally talk. She was willing to consider it. "I would assume it took him to its… home, or whatever," she said.

"I wonder where it lives," he said in a thoughtful voice.

Suddenly a scream broke through the night. Kate jumped into the tent without a second thought, and Roy Hastings scrambled to the rear of it. Miguel, Sam, and the two guides jumped up, their weapons and tranquilizer guns appearing like magic; they were on top of their game, all right.

The scream came again, then again. It sounded as if it was right overhead. Sam and the others were searching the night sky blindly with their eyes. Then the firelight illuminated the underside of the creature. It was flying in a circle over their camp.

It gave another scream, then something dropped from the sky. It hit the ground hard about ten feet from the fire, making the dust and leaves around it fly. The men were waving their weapons, and the bird screamed again before it flew off into the night. It continued to belt out its cries, and they grew more and more distant until they stopped altogether.

Sam ran to the pile that was lying on the ground just outside of the firelight. It had broken apart somewhat, and he didn't have to get right up on it to tell what it was. It was the bones and mangled head of Harold Kreiger. Sam cried out and jumped back, his hand over his mouth to still the sound of his own voice.

"What is it, Mr. Daniels?" Miguel was approaching Sam then. He knelt down and, just as Sam had, jumped up and back as if bitten by a snake. He too covered his mouth, but unlike Sam, he ran for a bush and vomited up the soup he had just eaten.

Hastings was sitting up now, rocking back and forth and covering his ears with his hands. Kate went to the door of the tent. "Sam? Sam? What the heck is it?"

Sam turned his back to the pile to see both Glaucio and Abilio still waving their weapons at the now-dead sky. He turned to Kate and shook his head. "It's what's left of Kreiger, Kate. The thing brought us back our own dead."

R.W.K. Clark

CHAPTER 21

It took Kate and Sam most of the night to get Hastings to the point of getting even the smallest amount of sleep. Even Miguel and the guides seemed unable to rest. Each of them tried to lie down a few different times, but each time they would get back up and join the others. Miguel finally gave Kate a handgun, and she made it a point to stick close to Hastings. It was the only way he was even the slightest bit calm.

He finally fell asleep around three in the morning. Sam tried to encourage Kate to rest as well, but she ignored his efforts. If the men couldn't sleep, how could they expect her to? Even Hastings was smart enough to fight slumber. This was no time to be caught napping, and every one of them knew it.

By the time the sun began to rise the guides were already packing up camp. Sam and Miguel used the rising sun to help them see as they cleaned up Kreiger's remains; then they dug a hole and buried him, marking the spot for future reference. Miguel said a few words in Portuguese over the dead man for good measure.

"Sam," Miguel began as they organized the gear. "Are you sure you want to go on?"

"Miguel, I don't want to go on; I have to go on," he replied. "Tours are happening in this jungle. We cannot let this happen to innocent people. The thing must be stopped."

The man nodded and said, "I am with you then. I know this jungle well, and now I feel it has been violated."

"Well," Sam replied. "I am pretty sure that this... thing... feels the same way about us."

Kate had woken up Hastings for the trip, and at first, the man refused to join them. When she pointed out that he would be staying there alone, he changed his tune quickly. She even got him to eat an energy bar and drink some water, telling him that without nourishment he wouldn't be able to keep up with them. It was all it took to convince him.

They set out east at seven that morning, in the same order, except for Hastings, who demanded that he be by Kate in the middle of the line. He was a shaken-up mess, and no one argued. They all knew he would be more of a burden on one of the ends than anywhere else.

About an hour into their trek Miguel spoke up from the front of the line. "I believe the thing has a nest near here."

That got Kate's attention. "Why do you say that, Miguel?"

"By the place where we found Rico; it was near here, and the thing brought the other guy back willingly enough. He would not fly far on a full belly, no? What living thing does? Yet he rid himself of Rico fast, and then this man too."

Abilio joined the conversation. "Maybe a cave, do you think?"

"No," Miguel replied. "It flies high, and it is large. This thing is nesting in the treetops, away from danger."

Kate thought about this, then said, "What are some tall trees around here?"

"Kapok tree," Miguel stated without hesitation. "Very tall, very old, and very strong. Tall kapok would keep it from sight. We need to be looking up at the tops of the kapoks." He held up his hand to stop the group, then walked up to one tree that seemed terribly high. He patted its trunk and turned to look at Kate and Sam. "Kapok tree."

Kate left her place in line and approached the tree as well. The trunk was massive and oddly shaped. She felt it with both of her hands and looked to its top. It spread out at the top, but she could see no nest, at least, nothing that was big enough to house the creature they were hunting.

"I agree with Miguel," she said simply. "Compared to the other trees, this seems the most likely. If it does nest in a tree, anyway."

Miguel gave a firm nod and turned to the others. "Yes. We will keep our eyes on the kapoks."

Kate spoke up. "Give me binoculars," she said. "I'm in the middle. I will watch the trees."

Miguel looked at Sam, who in turn shifted his eyes to Kate. "I agree, hon. I think it is the best way."

Abilio swung his pack off his back and pulled a pair of binoculars from the front zipper pocket. He handed them to Kate with a nod and took the pack back up. She adjusted them to her face and vision and took her place in line.

"Let's go," she said simply.

They continued their trek at a bit slower pace. For the next two hours, Kate kept her eyes on the sky, picking up her feet to keep from stumbling. She took note of smaller birds leaving and arriving at smaller nests, and it helped her to eliminate different nest types from her observations. Her neck ached and her eyes hurt, but she pressed on, keeping her thoughts on the prize.

At exactly ten forty, just after Miguel announced he was going to start looking for a place to have lunch, they took a curve on a clear trail that took them in a more easterly direction. Kate looked at three kapoks to the left, then turned herself to the right. What she saw stopped her in her tracks and took her breath away.

The first kapok tree she focused on held a massive nest, a nest like she had never seen in her life. From where she stood it looked as if the thing was easily big enough for a couple of humans to live comfortably in, and that had her attention, but what really grabbed her was the purple and blue bird that was landing in it. It perched on the edge of the nest and set its eyes on her and the others.

It didn't scream; it didn't swoop. It sat patiently, and it watched them. The darn thing was still full, but it was keeping its eye on them, and she was sure it had been the entire time they had been here.

"Guys," Kate said, her voice distracted. Miguel was still walking, but Hastings, Sam, and Abilio had stopped behind her. "Guys!"

Miguel turned on his heel, as did Glaucio. "What is it, Kate?" Miguel asked.

"I found him."

Sam was beside her in an instant, and he took the binoculars from her eagerly. He focused them and aimed them, and instantly his mouth dropped open. "Damn, there it is. It looks like it's watching us."

"Oh, it's watching us," Kate replied with a smile. "I'm willing to bet it has been the entire time we have been here."

Miguel was next to Sam right away. He took the glasses and looked as well, and a broad smile came over his face. "We found its home," he said with wonder.

"Yes, and I don't think it is aware of that," she said. "How could it be? It's hunting us."

Miguel took the glasses from his face. "How will we get it, Miss Kate?"

She looked at Sam and Miguel with a smile. "We will hunt it."

R.W.K. Clark

CHAPTER 22

For the next two hours, Sam and Miguel looked for an area which provided them with cover, while also allowing them to keep their eyes on the creature and its nest. They set up no tent or camp. Rather, they made sure they could all be comfortable while being underneath broad leaves, hidden from view as much as possible.

Hastings seemed to be coming apart. He became uncooperative and even combative at times. Kate tried to keep him settled by her side, and every now and then he would wind down for short periods, but he always got himself stirred back up again.

"Roy, we are going to come out of this on top," she told him at one point.

He had laughed at her, almost hysterically. "But how many of us will be killed before that happens?" Kate had not bothered to answer him.

The other four men found a massive tree, dead and lying nearby. It was hollowed out a good deal, and there was a large opening in the side of it. They were able to hide inside and watch the nest easily while Kate stayed hidden with Hastings. She had a handgun, and she felt completely safe.

∞

The bird left the nest and circled the area three times in the next two hours. Kate told the men, when they reported this to her, that it was a wonderful sight and they were to stay out of the thing's view. It was circling and trying to pick them up in its sights again. If it saw them, she said, if it was stalking them, she expected it would sit in its nest and wait for an ideal time to attack. It would attack only one at a time, she believed, so she made it clear how important it was to stay with someone, and to stay under cover.

"I… I need to use the bathroom, Kate," Hastings said at about one in the afternoon. "I've held it as long as I can."

She looked at him. "I'll turn away. Just turn your back to me as well."

He shook his head at her violently, his eyes squeezed closed. "No! I mean, I have to use the bathroom."

"Oh," she replied. She had about a quarter roll of toilet paper flattened out and tucked in her makeup bag. She dug it out and handed it to him. "I'll turn my back, Roy. I won't look; I promise."

"No, Kate. I'm not going in front of you."

Kate let out a huge sigh and poked her head out from under the greenery that hid them. "Go around behind where we are now, but no farther, Roy. No farther!"

He took the roll and stepped out and quickly ducked to the left and around to the rear. It was just too close.

He couldn't do this with Kate so close! He looked to the right, then the left again. There was a large tree that he could go behind. That would be fine.

Hastings dropped his pants and squatted, his eyes shifting from the right to the left and back again. It came easily, and soon he was cleaning himself up and coming out from behind the tree to head back to Kate. He had gone out of the range she had told him, but it was only a bit farther.

He just reached the foliage that hid Kate and was preparing to turn left when he was violently jerked upward. His mind was struggling with what happened; for some reason, he thought he caught his shirt on the branch of a tree, but suddenly his feet left the ground. He looked down in amazement, and that was when he saw the talons sticking out of the front of his chest, blood dripping freely from them.

Hastings screamed as loud as he could and looked up. The thing had him, and it was looking down at him with what looked to be a smile. They climbed higher and higher in the sky. The last thing he heard before he passed out was Kate's voice screaming his name over and over again.

∞

"It didn't scream!" Kate was saying as Sam held her tightly against his chest. "I didn't even hear it or see it coming."

Sam and Miguel had seen it. They saw the thing leave its nest and head directly to the spot where they had tucked Kate and Hastings away. They had tossed their binoculars at the guides and run for the foliage to protect the pair, but they had not been fast enough. The damn monster had swooped silently out of the sky and snatched up Hastings without so much as a peep.

All of them were in the tree now, and Miguel had his binoculars fixed back on the nest. Every now and then he saw the creature's head, or he would observe it jumping. Once he thought he saw a shoe fly into the air. "The thing eats once a day," he said in a distracted tone.

"It knows we are hunting it," Kate said then. "It knows we have found it."

Sam looked at her as if she had gone mad. "It's an animal. How could it know that? It would have to have reasoned it out. Think about what you are saying."

Kate turned to him, anger in her eyes. Her voice remained calm when she responded to him, however. "That's why it didn't scream."

Sam knit his brow; she was right. That thing had screamed the other two times it attacked. It had even screamed when it threw Kreiger's remains down on their camp.

But it hadn't screamed when it snatched up Hastings; not even so much as a peep.

Miguel, whose eyes were glued to the binoculars, said, "Well, we will find out soon enough if it drops this man's bones on us too. If it does that we will know for sure that what Miss Kate says is true."

She turned to him. "What do you see now, Miguel?"

"It has settled down. It hasn't done much now for about twenty minutes." He put the binoculars down and rubbed his eyes. "We are stuck here until we figure out what we are going to do."

He put the binoculars back up to his eyes. Kate turned away from him and put her mind on the situation at hand. The last two attacks had been during the daylight hours. As a matter of fact, so had the initial attack, the one in which Rico was killed. There had been no attacks at night.

Then she thought about the creature throwing the body into their camp in the night. Yes, it had been nighttime, but there had been a fire, and the thing had circled it several times.

"I don't think it can see well enough at night to attack," she said.

Sam turned to her. "But he brought Kreiger at night."

"Yes," Kate replied, "but we had a fire, and it circled before dropping him. Listen, it has eyes like a man, like a human. Humans can't see well at night either. Think about the information we do have; it makes sense."

Sam thought about her words. "You may be right, but what does this do for us? You think we should hunt it at night?"

"No," she replied. "I'm thinking about the tranquilizer guns; we have been ill-prepared. We have gotten farther and farther away from the SUVs. How long does one of those trank shots last?"

"For an animal that size? Four hours," Miguel said.

Kate shook her head in frustration. "The cage is in the car, you guys, and we are more than four hours from the cage. He won't be out long enough to get him back to the car."

Abilio's eyes grew wide. "I pump the thing with more than one! I do two or three!"

"But that could kill it!" Kate said, her voice raising. She turned to Sam. "Two of you are going to have to go at night and get the cage and bring it back here."

The men were all silent as they let the reality of what she said sink in. Finally, Sam spoke. "She's right. We have to go back for the cage. What time is it?"

Miguel glanced at his watch. "Nearly five thirty."

"Okay, okay," Sam continued. "Glaucio and I will go. We have guns and trank guns. We'll go at night, as soon as the sun is all the way down. Glaucio?"

The guide held Sam's eyes for only a minute before giving a firm nod. "I go."

"Sam?" Kate suddenly understood that he did not mean to send both of the guides, and her plan seemed impotent and stupid to her.

"Kate, you have to keep one of the guides here. I want to know you are safe, with the best."

She stared at him, tears pooling up in her eyes. She knew he was right. She closed her eyes, and the tears fell down her cheeks, but she nodded in agreement. "Fine."

For the next two hours, Sam and Glaucio checked over their weapons and discussed their plan. Glaucio told Sam he thought he could lead them through much faster by taking a different route, a direct route, and he pointed out that with only the two of them they would make far better time. By the time the sun was completely down Sam and Glaucio were armed and ready to go.

Sam sat next to Kate inside the tree and pulled her to him. She buried her head in his shoulder and clung to him tightly. "You have to come back, Sam. You just have to."

He pulled back and took her by the chin, tilting her head up in the light of the flashlight so he could see her face. "You better count on it. You're not going to get rid of me this easy." He kissed her long and hard then and embraced her as if it were the last time he ever would.

"Go," she said, pushing him away. "Go before I change my mind about all of this insanity."

He smiled at her and gave her one last kiss, then he and Glaucio stole into the Amazon night.

R.W.K. Clark

CHAPTER 23

Kate turned to Miguel in the darkness. She could only make out the shadows of him and Abilio, but their shadows were enough to make her feel safe. It was time to talk about the capture of the creature.

"Glaucio sounded like they would be back before sunup," she began. "Miguel, do you agree with him?"

She saw his head bob up and down, but only just barely. "The two men, Glaucio and Abilio, who have been with us, are the very best guides there are, Miss Kate," he said. "If he said they will make it, they will make it."

She took a deep breath. "Okay. How far can the trank guns shoot? Can we hit it from here?"

Miguel laughed. "If we could, I would have tried by now." He turned on the flashlight and aimed it away from the opening in the trunk. He then looked at Kate. "It is easier to talk if I can see you. We will need to get closer, and we will need to do it carefully."

"What will you do?"

He looked at her then, and his eyes became very serious. "We will bait it."

"What the heck do you mean, 'bait it'?" The words

no sooner left her mouth than something hit the tree. It jostled it just enough to scare the three inside into jumping.

Kate looked over at Miguel, panic in her eyes. "What the heck?"

Miguel turned off the flashlight. "That is your friend Hastings. It brought back our dead."

Kate closed her eyes. "It knows. It knows we are hunting it."

∞

Sam and Glaucio streaked through the night. They didn't have flashlights, but they did have neon sticks that gave off a soft glow. They kept those up their sleeves to use in emergencies, but the light of the moon was guiding them now. It was clear, and its brightness was sufficient.

They didn't speak; they only ran, walking only when they were in the thick. They seemed to be en route for only a couple of hours when Glaucio stopped him. He pointed to the north of where they stood. "That was where we first camped."

Sam could suddenly hear the waterfall, and a broad smile spread over his face. "You are amazing, man."

"I know," Glaucio replied. "Come on."

They took off again. If Sam's calculations were correct, they were going to be at the SUVs in no time. Sure enough, not ten minutes later he could make out the vehicles' bulky bodies. Without speaking the two men went to the second vehicle, the one Abilio and Glaucio had been in. It was the one with the cage.

Glaucio used his keys to open the back. When the interior light came on, he shut the door quickly. "We must get it from the inside."

"Why don't we just drive the car as far as we can, then take the cage the rest of the way on foot?" Sam asked.

Glaucio looked at him sheepishly. "Good idea."

The two men got into the vehicle and locked themselves in. Glaucio started the engine and slowly maneuvered it around the SUV in front of them, then he gave it gas. The headlights bounced to and fro off of trees and plants, but it lit up the trail wonderfully.

Within one hour Glaucio pulled the vehicle over and shut off the lights. "We are only about five hundred yards from the tree," he said. "We have to wait, though. It will surely have seen the lights. Let it lose track of us again in the dark."

The guide climbed over the seats and fiddled around in the cargo space.

"How long should we wait?" Sam asked.

Glaucio was squinting into the night sky. "We will wait for a quarter-hour," he replied.

When fifteen minutes passed the men got out of the vehicle, and Glaucio went around and pulled a folded metal cage out the back. It was large, but the fact that it folded flat would make carrying it easier than Sam had expected. He met Sam at the front of the car, where Sam took hold of one end of the metal contraption, and Glaucio took the other. "Ready?" Glaucio asked him.

"Let's go," Sam replied.

With that, the two men started running awkwardly in the direction of the tree.

∞

"Listen," Miguel said. "I hear something."

Kate and Abilio both looked skyward as they peeled their ears to listen. Kate could hear nothing, but she could tell by the look on Abilio's face that he was tuned into it. She strained even harder, and finally, she heard heavy footsteps and something metal rattling.

It was Sam and Glaucio.

The sun had just started to rise, and Kate had begun to panic. Now she felt a rush of relief like nothing she had ever experienced before. Miguel looked at her. "You stay here, Miss Kate." He slapped Abilio on the arm, and the two of them grabbed up their weapons and the flashlight and leaped from the hollow tree.

Kate poked her head up and out of the hole just in time to see Miguel and Abilio reach Sam and Glaucio. Sam and the guide stopped, and they were trying to pop the flat cage into shape. Abilio reached them and lent a hand, but it seemed that they were struggling.

Kate heard a rush of wind, and she looked up. There, swooping down in the sky, right toward the four men, was the creature. It made no warning sound, and it gave no scream. Just as it had done when it took Hastings, it swooped toward the men in an attack.

"No!" Kate screamed, and the men all looked up. The monster dug its clutches into Abilio, who immediately began to kick and fight. "Shoot it! Shoot it now!" Kate screamed.

As if on autopilot, Miguel lifted up his tranquilizer gun, aimed, and pulled the trigger. The dart flew and hit the thing just under its right wing, right in its breast. It gave a loud 'squawk!' and the flapping of its wings immediately slowed. Abilio was still kicking and had begun to scream. He continued to scream as the creature, now completely out of it, fell to the ground hard.

Sam, Miguel, and Glaucio, with guns and tranquilizers still in hand and aimed, ran for the still body of the creature. Abilio was lanced clean through by the thing's talons, and blood was pouring from him. Glaucio knelt next to his friend, who looked at him with wide, dying eyes.

"Me mata," the man said, his voice raspy and gurgling. "Me mata…"

Sam put his hand on Miguel's shoulder. "What is he saying?"

In response, Miguel lifted his handgun and put the nose of it against Abilio's temple. Abilio looked at the man, and his eyes softened.

Miguel pulled the trigger to the handgun, and Abilio's head blew apart. Miguel fell backward onto his rear and stared at the man. "He wanted me to kill him. Now we have to get him off that thing and get it in the cage."

Sam and Glaucio, jumped to action. They pulled the body of Abilio from the razor-sharp talons that had impaled him through and through, and then they dragged the sleeping creature to their cage. They locked it, and Miguel took a steel padlock and reinforced the unit.

"If it wakes, we shoot again," he said simply. "I will go get Miss Kate. You two put the cage in the back; put up the Plexiglas to separate. Glaucio, you know how."

Sam and Glaucio went to carry out the man's orders while he fetched Kate Beck and their gear.

"Did it kill him, Miguel?" she asked. "Is Abilio dead?"

He helped her from the tree and grabbed the two packs that were inside. He took the tent from one of them and looked at her as he turned to go back to the dead man. "I guess that Abilio was meant to be the bait," he said simply, and he dragged the canvas tent behind him to wrap up the body of the guide.

CHAPTER 24

"For the next six months, we will focus our studies on the archaeopteryx reptilious, or more commonly, 'Blood Feather.' At least, that is what it has been dubbed by the press." Dr. Kate Beck stood at the oak podium giving her first introductory lecture into the creature they had captured just three months before. "The archaeopteryx reptilious was discovered by photographer Samuel Daniels during a trek into the Amazon jungle. As you may or may not know, the species is terribly violent. The only living archaeopteryx resides here, at the university, and it is kept under close guard. It took four lives, very violently, I might add, before its capture."

She had the students' rapt attention, and she used it to her advantage. She spent the next half hour drilling into them the procedures used when dealing with the bird and even showed them photos of two of its victims so they would know the importance of following those procedures.

"It is believed that the archaeopteryx is not aviary, rather, it is firmly believed to be descended from dinosaurs," she continued. "We have theorized that its egg was somehow preserved and then hatched during an Amazonian earthquake."

Kate looked up at the clock on the wall. "Tomorrow we will actually venture over to the lab and give you all your first look. Keep in mind this is the only known specimen, so we want you to have the opportunity to study it, as we do not know its exact lifespan. Make sure to do your assigned reading before tomorrow, as it involves procedures. This is all about procedures, people!"

With a wave of her hand, she dismissed them, and they all stood and gathered their things like inmates that had just been set free. As they trickled out of the classroom, Kate grabbed her own bag and hung it on her shoulder, then turned out the main overhead lights and headed out of the room. She wanted to spend some time with Jason going over the agenda for the following day. After all, this would be the first class to study the creature officially, and it was a matter of life and death that they get it right.

She walked across campus to her lab. Since they had brought the thing back a lot had changed for Kate at the university. She now had her own class and curriculum. She found herself giving more magazine and television interviews, then she would have ever imagined.

Finally, she would be marrying Sam Daniels at the end of the year in Jamaica. Her life couldn't be more perfect if she personally tailored it from beginning to end.

Kate arrived at her lab and greeted Martha. "What do you have for me today?" she asked the receptionist.

"Well," Martha replied, "I could read it to you, but then you wouldn't get back to the lab before tomorrow. How about I just hand you the nice, neat list I made?"

Kate laughed. "It would definitely be more conducive to getting out of here at a decent hour, I'm sure." She reached across the woman's desk and took two full sheets of paper, casting a glance over them, and continued to her lab. "Have a good evening, Martha. It is nearly five, after all."

She heard the bird screaming and headed down the hallway without stopping at her office. Jason was seated about twenty-five feet from its containment unit. He had just fed it its dinner meal: an entire beef loin. It was tearing its claws into the meat and uttering screeches that were unearthly. Kate took her bag from her shoulder and left it near the door before making her way to Jason. He had a pair of protective earmuffs on, and he was writing furiously on his trusty clipboard.

Kate took hold of one side of the muffs and lifted it off his ear. "How's the baby, Jason?"

He rolled his eyes and put the clipboard down before removing his ear muffs. "A pain in my rear. Does nothing but scream all day, and I am positive it is planning my demise, even as we speak."

"Procedures, Jason," Kate said, looking the young man firmly in the eye. "Procedures."

She walked up to the metal bar that had been

installed shortly after 'Spike's' arrival; it was meant to show how close one could get to his containment unit and still be safe. "Hey, Spike," Kate said in a soothing voice. "How's your day?"

The creature stopped its screaming all at once, its eyes fastened firmly on Kate's own. Kate quickly looked away and walked up to the coat rack where her lab coat hung. Spike followed her with its eyes, never once taking them off of her. It then began to hum its warbling tune.

Kate put her lab coat on and turned to Jason, who had a funny look on his face. "You know, Kate, I have been down here with it all day, every day. This is the very first time it hasn't screamed all day long."

"Hmmm," she replied, thinking about what he said. She put on protective eye gear that blocked Spike's ability to 'lure,' or so it seemed. They worked, and wearing them was required. She walked back up to the rail and leaned against it, looking at the beautiful prehistoric creature before her.

Spike warbled and tilted its head from side to side, but Kate felt no effect. She studied its head movements and listened to its song for a moment before turning back to Jason. "You may as well get out of here," she said. "Sam won't be home until late, so I'll put some time in with old Spike here."

"Gladly." Jason stood and handed the clipboard over to Kate and took off his lab coat. "Guess I'll see you tomorrow. I'm gonna go catch a new movie. I've wanted to do it all week. Think I'll take advantage of the freedom." He gave Kate a pat on the back. "See you tomorrow," he said and left the lab.

She turned her attention back to Spike, who hadn't taken its eyes off of her. She smiled at it. "You sure can be a charmer when you want to be." She turned her attention to the clipboard to record its easy-going disposition. After all, it was unusual.

Kate began to pace along the length of the rail as she wrote. She was so focused on what she was doing that she took no notice of the small puddle of water on the floor. Her soft-soled shoe slipped off of it easily, and Kate's feet flew out from under her.

She would have been fine, had she not slipped under the rail. It was when you were on the other side of the rail that you were in danger. Spike's containment unit didn't protect you if you went under the rail.

That was just what she did. As soon as she realized that she was in the danger zone, Kate began to flail, struggling to get back on the other side. She almost didn't feel it when Spike buried its talons in her back and pulled her to the cage.

R.W.K. Clark

EPILOGUE

The blue Amazon sky complemented the emerald-green foliage that sprouted so freely and happily. There was a wonderful breeze, and the sound of the animals, birds, and insects gave the sense that this was heaven on Earth. True, there was no place like it.

A green-winged macaw swooped from a kapok tree and took flight in the sky. It was one of the clearest, most peaceful days the Amazon had had, free of rain and overcast. The bird was enjoying the fact that it was able to dance in the sun. It swooped to and fro, squawking with delight.

As the macaw flew it gained altitude, going higher, and higher, and higher still. Up ahead was a massive kapok tree, taller than all the rest. It set its sights for the tree and picked up speed. As it got nearer, it took note of the nest in the top. It would be a good place to rest.

The macaw landed on the lip of the nest, which was as big around as the treetop itself. It looked curiously at the contents of the nest. There were all kinds of things the bird didn't recognize, like bones, shoes, and some animal skeletons.

On the far side, there was a pile of feathers. They

were bright purple and blue, and they lay amidst a pile of bones.

About ten feet from the feathers there were three colorful balls, almost three-dimensional in appearance. The colors seemed to give the ball's depth. It was almost as if you could see right inside of them.

The macaw cocked its head with curiosity and waddled over to the balls, stunned by their beauty. It tapped its beak on one of them, then rolled it around slightly with its foot. Suddenly the ball jumped, and a crack formed along the side. The macaw was entranced. It moved closer to see what was happening to the pretty ball.

It split open, and a scream emerged from its guts. A long pointy beak emerged, and two bony hands ripped the rest of the shell apart, allowing the creature living inside to break free. It stretched and screamed, scaring the macaw with its loudness.

It moved around for only a moment before it took notice of the colorful bird standing before it, observing its struggles. It stopped screaming and stared the macaw in the eye. Soon, it began to warble a tune without rhyme or rhythm. The macaw thought it was the most beautiful thing it had ever heard. It must move closer. It must get close to the music, to the eyes, so it could see and hear it better.

Only a fraction of a second passed before the creature reached out with its bony hands and grasped the macaw, stabbing it with its talons and draining the life out of it. The poor bird twitched violently as it died, a reaction which ceased altogether when the creature buried its pointy beak through the center of the bird's body.

For the next fifteen minutes, the small creature feasted on the bird, its feathers, and its blood and bones. It then turned its attention to the other two eggs, one of which was beginning to hop around a bit.

The creature walked on unsteady feet to the moving egg. It gave a good jump, and a long crack formed. Right then the other egg began to roll back and forth slightly, and a light tapping began to come from the inside. The first creature watched with sapphire eyes, like the eyes of a human, as its brother and sister began their struggle to enter the world. It took its tongue and busied itself with cleaning its feathers off and fluffing them up as it watched the show. In no time at all the second egg was broken in two, and the second creature said hello to the world. It began to scream with hunger, its head moving back and forth as it tried to smell any food at all nearby.

The third egg took a little longer. The creature inside seemed weaker than the first two. The eldest, a boy, stood and watched as the newborn girl got closer and closer to the egg. She could smell the weakness of the boy creature inside. He wasn't strong. He was having a very hard time getting himself free. On three occasions the thing inside had to stop and recharge. He just didn't have it in him to do it all at once, as his siblings had.

The girl was losing her patience. She got right up on the egg and began to push at it with her pointy beak. It would roll a bit, then the creature inside would begin to struggle, and it would roll right back. It managed to get a small crack in the shell, but in its weakness, it could not completely break free.

Finally, the female creature, hungry and impatient, had had all she could take of watching her sibling fail. She drew back pecking hard with her beak at the shell. The shell cracked open. It split entirely and fell away, exposing the wet feathers of the male creature inside.

Now the girl began to warble, her head bobbing back and forth. She stared at the weak sibling, who hadn't been given the opportunity to fight, weakly fluttered and twitched. It looked at its sister with miserable eyes. It seemed to hurt all over. By denying it the much-needed exercise of breaking from the shell she had doomed it to death, and she knew it. She almost seemed to smile as she watched the struggle, as did the male behind her. Finally, she grew tired, and she uttered one long scream before she opened her beak and ripped her sibling's throat out. Finally, her first meal.

Welcome to the world…

ENTREATY

This book was made possible by reviews from readers like you. Reviews fuel my creativity. If you enjoyed this novel, I implore you to please write a review and share your experience on the retailer's website. The livelihood for authors is entirely dependent on reviews, and I must say, it is the largest obstacle as a struggling author that I have encountered. Please tell a friend, tell a loved one about this read. With your help, I will be one step closer to overcoming this obstacle. In return, I thank you from the bottom of my heart, and sincerely appreciate your time and effort.

Humbled, with gratitude,

R.W.K. Clark

ABOUT THE AUTHOR

I am a father of two beautiful children, Jon and Kim. They are my motivating forces; they are the lighthouse in this vast ocean. In my life, they are the air that I breathe; they are the oasis in this desert of uncertainty. They are my greatest joy in life and my number one priority. I have a long list of hobbies, and I attribute that to my lust for life! I like to surround myself with positive people, who share the same interests. Family values, the arts, outdoors, nature, and travel are tops on my list. I embrace attending cultural and artistic events because I believe dramatic self-expression is the window to the soul. I wear my heart on my sleeve, and I still believe in chivalry, and I always treat people the way I want to be treated.

www.rwkclark.com